HORSE COUNTRY

COUNTRY

No Place Like Home

Also by Yamile Saied Méndez

The Horse Country Series

#1: *Can't Be Tamed*

#2: *Friends Like These*

#3: *Where There's Smoke*

#4: *No Place Like Home*

Blizzard Besties

Random Acts of Kittens

Wish Upon a Stray

On These Magic Shores

Shaking Up the House

Copyright © 2023 by Yamile Saied Méndez
Interior art by Winona Nelson, © 2023 Scholastic Inc.

ISBN 978-1-338-74952-6

10 9 8 7 6 5 4 3 2 1   23 24 25 26 27

Printed in the U.S.A.   40
First printing 2023

Book design by Stephanie Yang and Omou Barry

For Chloe Turner, 4th grade

1

Trailblazing

Carolina Aguasvivas might have known every corner of Paradise Ranch better than the back of her hand, but the mountain trails around the property were a surprise every day.

Even though she never knew what to expect, she still felt at home in the wild. After all, it was where she'd grown up.

In early June, the trees and bushes burst with newness. The fresh green leaves showed nibbles from hungry deer, and the eagles glided over the canopies of the woods, searching for unsuspecting prey. The air smelled of rich earth, dew, and wildflowers.

Carolina watched for the unmistakable crimson shock of poppies that covered the burned patches of the forest like the prettiest kind of bandage. The world—at least this corner of it—had healed from the recent fires with a bloom.

She was lost in her awe of nature when Chelsie called from behind, "Watch out!"

Not a second too soon, Carolina snapped out of her thoughts and ducked so a tree branch wouldn't hit her in the face.

"Yikes," she exclaimed, holding on to the horn of the saddle to steady herself in case Shadow, the gray Arabian she was riding, got spooked by her outburst.

But Shadow stopped patiently, cool like Abuelita Ceci's strawberry and mint aguas frescas, Carolina's favorite summertime drink.

After pretending to wipe sweat off her forehead, she turned and waved over her shoulder. "Thank you, Chels!"

"You're welcome!" Chelsie replied, laughter in her voice.

"That was close!" said Abuela Ceci. She was riding Marigold, a sure-footed and calm mustang.

"You're supposed to be scoping the terrain, Caro," Chelsie said, still laughing. She was the caboose of their little train. "Stay in the present!"

Shadow nickered. It sounded like he was teasing Caro too. Typical Shadow!

"Stop it, you! This branch wasn't here yesterday!" she said, leaning forward and patting his neck. "You should've warned me, boy."

Carolina hadn't expected that seemingly overnight the tree branches would make an arch over the narrow deer path that led to Sleeping Princess Rock. The formation in the shape of a sleeping girl was a popular destination with tourists who traveled to this area of Idaho every year, especially during the summer and the fall.

She had been to the famous landmark once, but she'd been so young, her dad had held the reins of her horse on the long ride up the mountain. Abuela Ceci and Chelsie had never been. The trek wasn't for beginners, so they needed to build up to it. Putting into practice one of the Five Bs—Be focused—the trio was focused on reaching the top by the end of the summer. For that, they'd break it up into small goals. Today they wanted to cross the brook.

From the first day, Carolina had chosen Shadow for their

trail ride. Now, every morning, he eagerly waited for Carolina to tack him up. He was an excellent partner.

At first, they had taken the same route, but slowly, they'd ventured into new ones. Their horses, Shadow, Velvet, and Marigold, were more confident than they had been just a few days ago. Used to their endless chatter and Boo's occasional burst of barking when a squirrel or a bird crossed their path, the horses trudged determinedly even when the terrain was steep or surrounded by prickly bushes.

But at this pace, they'd be lucky just to make it to the babbling brook—that is, if they didn't want to be late for the next Unbridled Dreams student's first class. The barn's next sponsored student was ready to start the summer session, and the first day of lessons was always Carolina's favorite. They were all special, but Brielle might be their last scholarship student! Their current donor was only signed on to sponsor this last twelve-week program. If they didn't find a way to keep funding the lessons, then that'd be the end of Caro and Chelsie's dream to make the healing power of horses available to more people.

If this was the indeed the end of the road, had all the work and effort this last year been for nothing?

The thought made Carolina's mood turn gray like a storm cloud and her forehead bead with sweat. She wasn't the only one sweating though.

Although the temperature wasn't even in the high eighties yet—it took a while to warm up, even in the summer—Shadow and the other horses could do with a cool drink. The trail wasn't steep or difficult, but he was the one doing most of the work carrying her.

He snorted as if he could hear her thoughts. And considering how attuned the two had become in the last few months, that might have been almost true.

"You're right, Shadow," Carolina conceded, "I should've paid more attention." She gave her horse a pat.

Her horse was a figure of speech.

The horse she was riding was more accurate.

El Cabeza Dura, like she called the spirited and stubborn gelding, didn't belong to her, or even to Paradise Ranch, but he was always her first choice for any activity from trail riding

5

to galloping in the pasture and lessons in the indoor arena. They both preferred riding in nature to rules and judges or even ribbons. They made a good team.

Carolina was about to ask Shadow to walk on, when she remembered the duties of being first in a caravan, even if it was a small one like theirs. Everyone in their group had a job.

Boo, Caro's white-and-black spotted dog, ran ahead. The trailblazer scoped the path and made sure everything was safe. But as the first rider in line, Carolina still had to look out for what the trail had in store for the horses and riders behind her. From Shadow's perspective, things looked very different than from the saddle, and vice versa. She could hardly see the ground and she needed to trust him to be sure-footed, and in turn, he had to trust her to lead them in the right direction.

She signaled to Shadow to stand still just by sitting deeper in her saddle. Once she was sure he wasn't going to move, she grabbed the branch to move it out of the way and let her grandma and Chelsie walk through without being smacked.

But then, a thorn pierced her hand.

"Ay!" she exclaimed, and fought the urge to let go. She didn't want the thorny branch to hit her face when it sprang back.

Chelsie looked up, alarmed, and wiped a strand of stubborn hair out of her eyes with a hand. A gloved hand.

Unlike Carolina, who usually rode wearing a pair of jeans, a T-shirt, and cowgirl boots, Chelsie always wore her fancy practice outfits, including gloves to protect her just-manicured hands.

Horse girls came in every style, Heather, Chelsie's mom and the owner of the ranch, liked to say, and how right she was!

"Oh, mi amor, did you get poked?" Abuela Ceci asked, concerned.

Carolina was so glad her grandma was here with her!

Abuela Ceci, her dad's mom, had arrived by surprise last week.

The best surprise in the world!

For a split second, after the first hug and tears of happiness, Carolina wondered if it would be weird to get to know her grandma in person again. After all, they hadn't seen each other in over two years. This last year alone there had been so many changes.

When they had said their last goodbyes, Carolina had been in fourth grade and Paradise had been known as Orchard.

HORSE COUNTRY

BOOK 4
No Place Like Home

Yamile Saied Méndez

Scholastic Inc.

Now she was much taller and—she wanted to believe—wiser.

But Abuela Ceci was the same as always. Wonderful.

She noticed everything, not only about the terrain and the weather, but the animals, and things that Carolina hadn't known she had been keeping private.

Like now that she was trying to be brave and not cry over the thorn piercing through her hand. Abuela Ceci urged Marigold on until she was side by side with Shadow.

"Let me see," she said, taking Carolina's hand in hers.

She didn't wear gloves either, but she always wore a helmet. Hers was black with an Unbridled Dreams sticker on it. Her hands were soft but worn too. Her robin's-egg-blue nail polish was already chipped on her thumb.

"It doesn't really hurt," Carolina said. "See? It's not even bleeding. That much, at least." She wiped her hand on her jeans and shrugged, but her hand throbbed, contradicting her words.

"You still need to wash it and put antiseptic on it as soon as we get back. It's a wild apple tree. Didn't you notice, sweetheart?"

Now that Carolina looked at the tree with attention, she realized that Abuela Ceci was right. Of course.

"I'll be more careful next time," Carolina said. "I just wasn't expecting to find an apple tree in the middle of the trail."

"Good point," Abuela Ceci said. "Apples, like peaches and most fruit trees, or even those poppies we saw, aren't native to this area. But remember that when the pioneers crossed the plains and headed to the west coast, they planted trees for those who'd come after them."

"Like Johnny Appleseed," Chelsie said.

They'd had breakfast this morning (pancakes, eggs, and bacon), but the mention of fruit made Caro's mouth water and her tummy rumble.

She wasn't the only one who was always ready for a snack.

Shadow had taken the opportunity to munch on some grass.

"Stop eating that, Shadow." Carolina gently pulled on his reins and motioned for him to get going. "You're going to get a tummy ache, and I'm telling you right now, I'm not cleaning up your mess."

Shadow took one more bite before tossing his silver mane.

Chelsie laughed. "You say that now, but then you're the one spending the night next to him to make sure his stomachache doesn't turn into colic, right, Abuela?"

Carolina shuddered at the C-word. Colic is the boogeyman of stables.

"Right, mi amor!" Abuela said, and sent one of those glowing smiles Chelsie's way before they continued their ride.

Carolina felt a prickle in her heart. Not because her friend wasn't right. She had slept next to Shadow's stall a couple of nights ago, but it had been an accident. She'd just been worried about him. And yes, tired.

Chores at the barn were always demanding, especially so in the warmer months. Now that Tyler was back from college for a few weeks, she did have extra time for fun things like the ritual morning trail rides.

But she still felt prickly like the apple tree. She couldn't shake off the fear that all their work to build Unbridled Dreams would be for nothing if the sponsor didn't extend their generosity—or if they couldn't find anyone else to take their place. She sighed, trying to breathe out her unease and inhale peace.

Unfortunately, at the same moment, Shadow stopped for a potty break—the advantages of being a horse. Carolina's nose wrinkled at the scent of urine. She wanted him to quickly move out of the stinky spot, but Shadow was resisting going downhill, although the slope wasn't that steep.

She made kissing noises and tapped him with her heels, until he finally got going again.

Meanwhile, Chelsie had resumed the conversation that had been cut off by the thorny branch's sudden attack. "I guess in a way, I'm glad I don't have to sacrifice my summer, but I miss my dad."

Carolina loved summer, but she would've sacrificed all the summers in the world to be with her parents. Carolina knew Chelsie had felt super torn—she'd heard enough of her friend's indecision to know she was just saying this to make peace with her situation.

Chelsie's parents had recently divorced, and her dad, Milo Sánchez, had moved back to his birth country, Argentina. He was a famous polo player and was now an even more famous horse trainer. This was the first summer Chelsie was spending without him.

Abuela Ceci said, "It's hard to live far from loved ones."

Carolina turned to look over her shoulder and catch the loving smile she knew her grandma was sending her.

"And if it's harder than you imagined, talk to your parents. I'm sure the distance is hard for your dad too." Abuela always knew what to say.

An alarm chimed.

The horses' ears swiveled toward Chelsie's watch like little antennas.

"Time to go back," Chelsie said with a sigh.

"But we didn't even make it to the spot we reached yesterday!" Caro exclaimed, disappointed.

The girls looked up toward Sleeping Princess Rock. It seemed unreachable.

"Aren't we supposed to get better instead of worse?" Chelsie whined.

"Little by little, we'll make better time," Abuela Ceci said in a comforting way. "Sometimes you have to step back so you can assess and advance."

Carolina knew she was right, but she couldn't wait to see what the world looked like from the top of the mountain. She couldn't wait to see if up close, the rock really looked like the sleeping princess from the legend that Michael the farrier had told the girls last time he'd been around.

"Don't look so sad," Abuela Ceci said. "Your new student will be here soon."

The girls exchanged an excited look. Carolina felt like she had bubbles in her blood that rose to her head and made her giddy.

Boo, who must have heard the alarm, turned around before a bend in the trail and dashed back to the caravan. His little black eyes shone with mischief and his tongue lolled from the corner of his doggish smile. His fur was all wet and his paws muddy.

"Someone had fun rolling in the mud it seems," Abuela Ceci said, and the girls laughed.

They trekked back together and when they reached the last line of trees and saw the beautiful big barn, Abuela Ceci make a kissing sound and Marigold quickened her pace into a trot and then a canter.

Chelsie said, "I hope Marigold isn't too tired for Brielle's lesson."

As if she wanted to prove to Chelsie that a leisurely ride

in the mountains was no match for her, the yellow mustang tossed her mane and quickened her pace. Or had that been Abuela Ceci who had urged the horse to show off?

"Yeehaw!" exclaimed Caro's grandma.

"She's going to be just fine," Carolina said, laughing.

2

Fun, Rewarding, and Stylish

After the horses got a drink at the automatic watering trough that Carolina's dad had set up, Abuelita Ceci dismounted gracefully and tied Marigold to the post with a manger tie, a bowknot. This was an easy knot for a human to untie, but not so for a horse, which made it perfect for the barn.

"Thanks for the ride, Marigold. Have fun in your class," she said to the mustang, and planted a kiss on her nose. Then she looked at the girls. "I'll go up to the house for a bit. You girls okay taking care of the horses?"

"Of course!" they said in unison as Caro's grandma quickly walked uphill.

"What do you think she'll make for lunch?" Chelsie asked.

"Something delicious, that's for sure," replied Caro, her mouth watering at the promise of lunch.

But first, work.

Untacking the horses, brushing them, and cooling them down was part of the ritual of riding. Carolina never resented chores, although, sometimes, they were tedious. During the winter there was not much else to do, but in the summer, she'd rather be riding, swimming in the creek, or maybe just watching TV in the air-conditioning. But she would do anything for the animals to be happy. Plus, summer days are long, and Caro usually still had time for all those things after doing her work.

Summer itself went by so fast though! She had to make an effort to stay in the present and enjoy it. She squashed the little hint of sadness that reminded her of how quickly the fall would show up.

The sight of Tyler training Sterling, a beautiful silver dappled Morgan gelding, in the outdoor ring brought a smile to her face. Carolina was in love with the horse's unmistakable elegant gait.

Tyler had grown up in Paradise, but last year, he'd been at

college in Boise. He wanted to be a vet. In his teenage years, he'd been a troublemaker until horses changed his life. He'd taught Carolina a lot about horses and second chances. She loved him like an older brother and was happy he was back. At least for the summer.

"Hey, Tyler!" She waved in his direction.

"Hi, Caro!" two voices replied—Tyler's and Jaime's.

Carolina hadn't seen Jaime sitting, in the shade, on top of the fence around the ring, watching Tyler and Sterling learn how to communicate without words.

Jaime was almost fourteen, two years older than the girls. Like Caro, he had a birthday at the end of July.

Seeing him, Carolina's heart burst with happiness. Not because she had a crush on him or anything like that. But if Jaime was here, then Vida, his cousin and Carolina's best friend, had arrived too.

Then the boys called out again. "Hi, Chelsie!"

Carolina turned on the saddle to look at Chelsie's reaction. A few months ago, Chelsie had a major crush on Jaime. She never talked about him much, but Carolina didn't know if Chelsie was over him or not.

Now she didn't look bashful at all as she waved back and said, "Hi, Tyler and Jaime!"

The girls dismounted. Carolina looked over her shoulder and called, "And get to work, Jaime! You don't get paid to sit!"

"Yes, boss lady!" the boy replied, jumping from the fence and running in their direction.

"Wow! I didn't know I had such power over him!" Carolina laughed, loving the way he'd called her boss lady, even if it was just to tease her.

Chelsie nudged her with an elbow, deflating Caro's growing ego, and said, "Yikes. Why did you do that? Now he's coming over. How embarrassing!"

"I didn't think he'd come this way! I thought you wanted to talk to him."

But Chelsie wasn't angry.

"Not anymore, Caro!" she said, draping an arm over Caro's shoulder as they watched Jaime take the long way around the ring. "That's in the past. But since he sort of guessed that I liked him and never got the memo that I don't anymore, now it's kind of embarrassing to be around him."

Carolina clicked her tongue. "Get over it, Sánchez! You'll

bump into him all summer, so . . . Think about it as ripping off a Band-Aid."

"Speaking of Band-Aids," Chelsie said, taking Caro's hand in hers and inspecting the thorn poke. "Remember to wash your hands and put an antiseptic on it before it gets infected."

"Pshaw!" Carolina shrugged. "It was just a tiny thorn." The throbbing had turned into pain even though she tried to ignore it. Teasing, she said, "And you need to put some sunscreen on your nose."

Chelsie's hands flew to her face as she exclaimed, "Oh no! I forgot! I'm going to get freckles!"

Chelsie's freckles looked adorable. They made constellations over the bridge of her nose. For some reason, Chelsie didn't like them though.

Jaime met them just outside the big barn. "Here. I can take them from you," Jaime said, knowing the girls were headed for the spacious wash stalls. When he glanced at Chelsie, he blushed.

Did *he* have a crush on Chelsie now that she'd gotten over him?

Problems of the heart were so complicated. Which is why

after her crush on Rockwell, their previous student, had faded a little, Carolina vowed to never have another crush again.

"Here," Caro said, handing her reins to Jaime.

Chelsie smiled at Jaime a little shyly but held on to Velvet as they headed into the barn aisle. Jaime led Shadow, and Caro followed Chelsie and Velvet to the side-by-side wash and groom stalls.

Quietly, each of them enjoying the familiar tasks, Chelsie and Carolina unsaddled Velvet. They each got a body brush and carefully checked that the mare had no scratches from the trail that could get infected.

"Remember to check for ticks, Jaime," Caro reminded him.

"Got it," he said.

Ticks and lice that plagued the deer in the area could also infect horses and people and make them very sick.

After they'd checked Velvet, the girls checked themselves.

"Clear!" Carolina said, inspecting Chelsie's back like her eyes were super scanners. Then they switched.

"Clear!" Chelsie echoed.

They high-fived each other. Now that they were done

beautifying the horses, it was time to turn them out to the pasture for the rest of the day. Just hanging out was the horses' favorite pastime.

As if telling the kids to hurry, Shadow flicked his tail, which smacked Jaime's face. The boy's reaction was so dramatic it was ridiculous. He covered his forehead with his hands and exclaimed, "Ah! You vicious beast!"

Shadow snickered.

The three kids laughed. Shadow looked like he was smiling too.

On top of being stubborn, he was also handsome. With the new green shoots that grew in the pasture, the warm sunshine and the daily exercise, his beauty increased day by day.

Carolina wasn't vain, but she hoped that she was also having the same results from fresh food, sunshine, and exercise. She had grown so much this year, a few days ago her mom had ordered a bunch of clothes for her. More of the same things Carolina wore every day, just larger sizes. Still, she was excited to get her new clothes.

Chelsie too was excited.

For different reasons, this was the first time both girls were here for the new student's first lesson, and they were giddy to meet Brielle.

All they knew about her was that she had moved from Las Vegas to Paradise last winter. She attended the McAllister Elementary School, a couple of towns over, so the girls hadn't met her in school.

"Ready to share the juiciest gossip with your BFF?" Chelsie asked Velvet.

Velvet snorted and bobbed her head in excitement.

"Is Shadow heading out too?" Jaime asked. "I can take them both if you want."

"We'll do it," Chelsie said. "Thanks."

Jaime stayed in the stalls to hose them down and the girls led the horses toward the pastures.

Carolina said, "Let me put a fly mask on Shadow. Otherwise, the flies drive him nuts and at night he's grumpy."

Chelsie handed her one of the many mesh masks they kept in a box next to the pasture gate.

"He looks like a luchador!" Chelsie said as Caro Velcroed it over his face.

Shadow sent her a killer glare through the black-and-yellow mask.

"Don't be mad at me, Shadow," Chelsie said. "It was a compliment."

But he was already trotting away from them. Carolina narrowed her eyes, trying to see if he was limping, or if it was a trick of her eyes. But when he took off in a gallop toward the shady willows, there was nothing suspicious in his gait and she sighed in relief.

As usual, Leilani, a trusty quarter horse who was Velvet's best horse friend, was waiting for her by the salt block, swishing her tail. She neighed as if telling Velvet to hurry up.

"I wonder what they're going to talk about," Chelsie said.

"I'm sure Velvet is dying to tell Leilani all the gossip about Shadow's loud and smelly tooting on the way back." Carolina waved a hand in front of her nose.

They laughed and watched Bella, the painted miniature horse, butting in between Velvet and Leilani as if she didn't want to miss any of the gossip.

"Let's head to the little barn to see if Vida is there," Carolina said. "Brielle will be here any moment." Excited butterflies tickled her stomach.

"Let's hurry then!" They ran to the little barn where they had a stash of the essentials, including sunscreen and antibiotic ointment, along with drinks. A Velvet Lilly song rang out from the boombox. Carolina was smiling already, but as soon as they crossed the door, a pungent whiff made her nose wrinkle and her eyes itch.

What was that smell?

Her first reaction was to sniff her underarms.

"It's not you," Chelsie said with a chuckle as she turned the music down a little bit.

"The bedding in the minis' stall needed to be completely turned over," Vida said, walking out from the last stall in the hallway.

With a dramatic flourish, she placed the rake she was using up against the wheelbarrow full of soiled bedding, and wiped her forehead with her forearm. "Whew! That was hard but I did it!"

Carolina and Chelsie clapped, and Vida gifted them an elegant curtsy.

"Thank you, thank you," she said.

"Look at you!" Carolina exclaimed, and Vida beamed at her.

She had started horse handling and riding lessons just a couple weeks before, although not as a scholarship student. After years of watching Carolina from afar, she'd taken the plunge—along with a stronger prescription of her allergy medication—so they could all ride together during the Paradise parade at the end of summer.

At first, Carolina had worried that the only reason Vida had finally decided to take lessons was to make Carolina happy. Carolina wanted Vida to ride because she loved it too. And although she'd only just started, she seemed to be having fun. Sometimes it still didn't feel real to Carolina that her BFF had seriously joined Paradise!

Vida looked stylish in denim overalls and a white T-shirt underneath. Her muck boots matched her rainbow-streaked hair, which was back in a ponytail. If Unbridled Dreams got another sponsor and continued, Carolina would make sure they made brochures that showed that mucking the stalls could be fun, rewarding, and stylish—with Vida on the cover.

"Are you almost done?" Chelsie asked.

"Not quite," Vida said.

"That's okay!" Carolina said. "We'll help you later. Come to Brielle's first lesson with us. It will be a good refresher for you!"

"Sounds good!" Vida replied, setting down the pail she'd been carrying toward the big stall.

Luna, the gray tabby cat who ruled the little barn, moved from the patch of sunlight to a shady spot next to the sink as if she wanted the girls to know she'd keep them to their promise to clean the cat's kingdom.

"We'll be back, Luna!" Chelsie said, giving the cat an affectionate pat on the head. "You know we will."

"What happened to your hand?" Vida asked, concerned.

Carolina realized she'd been nursing her hand as if it were a wounded nestling. "Oh, nothing. Just a thorn."

"Let me see."

Vida took her hand before Carolina could stop her. She inspected the wound and pressed her mouth in a tight line as she softly brushed a finger over Caro's thumb. "The thorn is still there. If we had tweezers—"

"No!" Caro said, snatching her hand and hiding it behind her back.

"You should take care of it before it gets infected though. Even a tiny poke like that can become bad news if you leave it unattended."

"I already told her that," Chelsie said, "but did she listen? No."

Carolina rolled her eyes.

"It's because we love you," Vida said. "At least wash it."

Just then, the sound of a car's wheels crunching on the gravel interrupted them.

And with that, the rest of the chores and the splinter in Caro's finger faded to the back of her mind.

"She's here!" the three girls exclaimed, jumping in the air, and ran out.

3

A Meeting of Souls

Brielle Stuart and her mom got out of their white car, matching smiles lighting up their faces. Wide, friendly, genuine. Mrs. Stuart's lips were a bright pink that complimented her dark skin, along with her flowery silk top and bejeweled sandals. Brielle wore the light pink Unbridled Dreams T-shirt from the welcome package Kimber had mailed, stretchy riding pants, and brown cowgirl boots! Two adorable puffs peeked out from under her pink cap, which had the logo of McAllister Elementary School.

Carolina loved her immediately.

"Woah," Vida said, "I like her style."

"Me too!" Caro grinned.

"This is going to be the best summer ever," Chelsie whispered with badly contained excitement as the mom and daughter duo walked toward them.

"Hey!" everyone said in a chorus. Their voices had different pitches, but curiously enough, they harmonized.

They all laughed as they shook hands. After an awkward handshake with Rockwell, Carolina had made sure to up her handshake game. She was satisfied that now hers hadn't been either extra firm or limp like a cold fish.

"Hi, Vida." Brielle smiled, confident and outgoing. "I'm so happy you're here too!"

"Where do you two know each other from?" Kimber asked, voicing the curiosity burning inside Carolina.

"The pool and the community center!" Vida said.

They were all going to get along great!

"Brielle has been waiting for this day for weeks and weeks," said Mrs. Stuart. "Thank you for the opportunity!"

"Thank *you*!" Kimber exclaimed. After so many hours under the sun, her skin was dark gold and red glinted in her long braid. "We've been excited too!"

"Are those the horses?" Brielle asked, shading her eyes as she gazed toward the pasture in the distance. "They're all so beautiful!"

Vida nodded. The same look of adoration crossed Brielle's and Vida's faces.

Chelsie and Carolina beamed at each other.

"That's them, the stars of our program. The horses!" Kimber said. "Today you will work with Marigold. She's already waiting for us in the indoor arena."

"Am I going to be riding inside?" Brielle asked.

"We'll actually head to that ring," Kimber said, pointing toward the area where Tyler had been training Sterling. The Morgan horse was now in the pasture hanging out with Shadow.

The trees around the outside ring offered some much-needed shade. There was a new-to-the-ranch picnic table that Carolina's dad had set up just a few days ago so the parents could wait during their kids' lessons. Right now Tessa's mom, Mrs. Wilson, was sitting there since her daughter was finishing with Apollo.

Life at the ranch was busy in the summer! Everyone wanted to fit in as many lessons as possible, especially with all the equitation competitions coming up.

"Wow!" exclaimed Mrs. Stuart, placing a hand over her heart. "That's a gorgeous horse!"

Chelsie and Carolina nodded. Every time they passed Apollo, they both swooned at how pretty he was.

Starry-eyed, Brielle asked, "What kind of horse is he? Do I get to ride on him one day?"

Vida cleared her throat and Carolina thought she heard her say "Never," but she couldn't be sure. She nodded in agreement. Tessa was so selfish. She would never allow anyone but perhaps Tyler and sometimes Jaime to come close to her precious horse. But Chelsie gently elbowed Caro, as if to remind her to keep her tongue in check.

Tessa was Loretta's best friend. And Loretta was Carolina's archnemesis. Carolina had . . . opinions about them, but she wasn't about to start with the drama on Brielle's first day.

"He's a red roan Tennessee Walker Horse," said Chelsie, opting to answer the first half of Brielle's questions.

"Walker horse?" Brielle asked. "He sure can run though."

Apollo was galloping around the ring as if he was about to take flight. He was an older horse, in his twenties, but he was still fast and agile. He was a joy to watch, and Carolina imagined he'd be an even greater joy to ride. Not that she'd ever know with Tessa guarding him like a hawk.

"Horses that have the word *walker* in their breed can still move at other speeds," Chelsie added, laughing good-naturedly. "It's just because their walking style is very distinct."

Brielle bit her lip and scratched her head.

"So many new things to learn!" Mrs. Stuart said, smiling.

Carolina could imagine how Brielle must be feeling. Sometimes she felt intimidated at school, especially in movement class when she'd had to learn a dance.

"Don't worry about all the details," Vida said, draping an arm over Brielle's shoulders. "You'll learn soon enough. In any case, it's not like there's a test or anything." She looked at Carolina and Chelsie for confirmation.

"No! No tests!" Carolina said.

"At least not now," Chelsie replied, ignoring the look Carolina was sending her. Then she crossed her arms and added, "Unless you continue on to advanced lessons and then would like to compete."

"There's no competitions anytime soon," Caro hurried to say, worried Brielle would be anxious.

Carolina and Chelsie both loved horses, but they had grown up relating to them in very different ways. For Caro, they were always there, homey and safe. For Chelsie, they meant time for sports, training, and competitions. They didn't know yet what Brielle would want.

"Brielle is very motivated by challenges," her mom said. "Give her a goal, and she will work hard for it."

"Excellent!" said Kimber. She waved for them all to follow her to the indoor arena as she continued. "Having specific goals is one of our Five Bs, our guiding principles. We'll tell you all about them."

"You're staying, right, Ma?" Brielle looked over her shoulder toward her mom.

Mrs. Stuart addressed Kimber. "Okay if I sit there in the shade?" She motioned to the picnic table where Tessa's mom was sitting. "It's a long drive back to McAllister. By the time I get there, I'd have to head back."

"Of course!" Kimber said. "Make yourself comfortable either inside or outside."

With relief, Mrs. Stuart headed to join Tessa's mom, and the girls followed Kimber inside the arena, where Marigold was patiently waiting.

After their trail ride, Tyler had seemingly taken care of her—she'd been watered and unsaddled—but she seemed ready to keep going, even though it was hot. She was so different from some of the other horses! After a morning ride, Pepino only wanted to rest for the remainder of the day. Or the week!

"Oh!" exclaimed Brielle when she saw the dun mustang. "She's so pretty!" She carefully stretched out her hand, and Marigold turned her neck for Brielle to pet her. A few heartbeats later, girl and horse were nose to nose.

Something magical happens when a horse and a person exchange a breath. It's like their souls are meeting. And this seemed to be the case with these two.

Chelsie pressed Carolina's hand, excited. They couldn't have asked for a better start to the program.

Finally, Brielle blinked as if she were waking up from being hypnotized. She glanced up at Kimber and the girls who watched her, honoring this first encounter with a horse. Carolina thought that if this brief moment was all Brielle remembered from her first lesson or even the program, then they could call it a success.

If only Unbridled Dreams could continue forever!

"What kind of horse is she?" Brielle asked.

"She's a rescue from a wild herd in southern Utah, right, Kimber?" Vida said softly, coming up to Brielle's side and brushing her hand over Marigold's dark brown mane. The coarse hair was shiny and supple. A strong musky scent enveloped the horse after her exercise in the morning, one of Carolina's favorite scents.

"That's right," the trainer said.

Even though Vida had just started lessons, she was already eager to share what she'd learned so far. Carolina found her mind suddenly spinning with possibilities. What if in the future they asked other Unbridled Dreams students to become mentors to the new students? It could be part of the program's requirements like mucking the stalls and grooming the horses. They could even expand to offer more advanced lessons— and then those students could help walk the newcomers through all the information!

Carolina and Chelsie loved mentoring, but they couldn't be present at every lesson. It made sense to find new ways to keep the graduates involved so the skills they'd learned got extra practice.

So many ideas. So little possibility of them becoming a reality, though.

At least no one noticed that Carolina's mind was running frantically like a rat in a maze, trying to find solutions for problems too big for her.

The others were talking about the herd of wild horses Marigold had come from.

"Wild horses?" Brielle asked. "My brother just did a report on them for his second-grade science assignment! My mom found a booklet online that said that every year the BLM does a roundup. Is she from one of those?"

"BLM?" asked Chelsie, confused.

"The Bureau of Land Management," Carolina explained.

Michael had promised to take Carolina to southern Utah to see the bands of wild horses that lived in Glen Canyon. They lived in the most unreachable mesas and could only be seen from helicopters. One day . . .

"Mustangs are wild, but they come from domesticated Spanish horses, right?" Brielle asked.

"Mustangs are feral, not wild," Vida said nonchalantly, earning a look of respect from Chelsie.

"That's true!" Carolina exclaimed, delighted.

"I looked it up," said Vida, pretending she was brushing dust off her shoulder.

Kimber looked impressed that Vida and Brielle already cared enough about horses that they'd gone searching for information. "You're both right. Horses are feral in the sense that they come from domesticated animals, unlike a cougar, say, which is a true wild animal. But feral horses are called wild, nonetheless. Wild horses, specifically mustangs, are a symbol of America."

"The continent or the country?" asked Carolina, smirking.

"The country." Vida smirked back.

The girls argued constantly about the proper use of America.

Chelsie and Carolina, with family in South America, claimed it represented the whole continent, and Vida and Bracken, Caro's little shadow, said it meant the US.

"How old is she?" Brielle asked, brushing a hand over Marigold.

"She's about ten years old, and for having been feral *or* wild, she's kind and patient," Kimber said.

Everyone at Paradise loved Marigold.

"Mustangs are hardy and so smart," Carolina said. "That's why she's perfect for a first lesson. After today, you'll be in love with her forever."

"I am already in love with her!" Brielle exclaimed, looking at Marigold with adoration.

To save them time, Kimber had kept the tack nearby. It was only a matter of brushing her, then getting her pad and saddle back on.

"After the lesson, we'll give her a good refreshing bath," Kimber said.

Brielle nodded, attentive. Carolina imagined her head was like a sponge, absorbing all the information she could.

"Questions?" Kimber asked, after they went over the non-negotiable rules. Safety was the most important, so the top of the list was always wearing a helmet and never riding without supervision.

"That makes sense," Brielle said, her eyes flitting to the outside ring, impatient to go riding already.

Carolina understood the feeling. She'd just been on a long trail ride, but she never got tired of time on the saddle. When the weather was as glorious as today, wasting it was a crime.

"Let's go," Kimber said, gesturing with her head.

Brielle held on to the reins, the blazing smile still on her face. She waved to her mom when they walked past the picnic table. Mrs. Wilson had left; most likely she was helping Tessa groom and untack Apollo. She might be a grown woman, but once she'd told Carolina she was still a horse-crazy young girl at heart.

If only Tessa had a pinch of her mom's niceness, they could've all gotten along marvelously.

Mrs. Stuart wasn't alone at the picnic table though. Abuela Ceci had brought a pitcher of her famous aguas frescas and was happily chatting with Brielle's mom. She smiled at the girls when they sat at the table.

Mrs. Stuart and Abuela Ceci watched attentively too, silent so as not to distract rider or horse. Vida quietly took her phone out from her pocket. At first Carolina had the impulse to tell her to put it away, that this wasn't the time to scroll through her social media. But Vida was taking pictures and videos of Brielle.

"Great idea!" Chelsie said, her eyes wide.

Kimber went through the basics of creating a relationship with the horse before the rider even sits in the saddle.

"Brushing her and tacking her up already showed her that you care about her as an individual," Kimber said. "The relationship is based on mutual trust. She's a powerful animal, hundreds and hundreds of pounds. But she's also very vulnerable. She's trusting that you will know what to do, where to guide her, and not to hurt her."

Carolina's heart about melted when Marigold snorted in agreement.

The trainer continued showing Brielle how to lead Marigold through the different gaits (walk, trot, canter, and gallop) from the ground, with Marigold traveling a wide circle around them.

She showed Brielle how to join up with Marigold. Done with her warm-up, Marigold recognized Brielle's body language and walked to join her in the middle of the circle. Marigold's neck wrapped around Brielle.

"Aw," Mrs. Stuart said, as if she too could imagine the softness of a horse embrace.

Vida shuddered. "It does feel nice, but sometimes I'm scared the horse will step on me!"

"That's why you always make sure to wear boots," Abuela Ceci said, patting Vida's shoulder.

Finally, now that Marigold and Brielle were connected like old friends, it was time for Brielle to get on the mounting block and ride.

"She's fearless!" Carolina exclaimed when Brielle swung onto the saddle in a smooth arc.

"Let's go on a walk around the ring," Kimber said, holding the lead rope like she was taking a giant dog for a stroll.

Things were going well until Brielle seemed to become distracted. Her eyes flickered to the trees around the ring, the still white-capped mountains in the distance, and an eagle soaring above them.

Sensing her distraction, Marigold slowed down to a stop.

"Why is she stopping?" Brielle asked, dismayed. Gently, she nudged Marigold's sides with her heels. The mare obediently resumed her walk.

"She thought you wanted to stop to gaze at your surroundings," Kimber said.

"For real? Like, can she read my mind?" Brielle asked.

"In a way, yes, she can. She reads your emotions. Let's do an experiment. Without signaling with your legs, hold the reins softly and think about heading to that barrel at the other end of the ring," Kimber said. She unhooked the lead rope from Marigold's bridle and got out of the way.

After a couple of seconds in which Marigold just stood patiently, the mare took a tentative step, and then walked straight toward the barrel.

"Wow!" Mrs. Stuart said again.

"This is perfect!" Carolina whispered to Chelsie. "She's a natural!"

Vida smiled but her cheeks flushed bright red.

Did she think Brielle was a better rider than her?

Just then, Marigold started trotting, catching Brielle off-balance.

"Oh no!" Vida exclaimed.

As if they were synchronized windup toys, Chelsie and Carolina jumped to their feet, ready to run to Brielle's rescue.

4

First Things First

Everyone around her was panicking ... but Brielle couldn't stop laughing.

Marigold had skidded to a halt, which knocked Brielle farther to the right. Holding on to the saddle horn for her life, she hollered, "Catch me if I fall!"

Marigold flicked her tail as if she were trying to swat a pesky fly.

"Don't worry," Abuela Ceci whispered to Mrs. Stuart. "Kimber is an expert instructor. She has everything under control."

And it was true. In a couple of seconds, Kimber had helped Brielle straighten up as if nothing had happened.

"Let me see if I need to tighten the cinch a bit," Kimber said.

Without missing a beat, Brielle moved her leg just the way Kimber needed. Once the trainer had made sure the cinch was tight enough, Brielle resumed her slow walk around the arena.

The pink flush slowly left Mrs. Stuart's face now that it looked like her daughter was okay.

Slowly, trying not to startle Marigold or her rider, Chelsie and Carolina sat down, relieved. They both took the cups of aguas frescas Abuela Ceci handed them as if she knew how their mouths and throats had gone dry with the fright.

A few months ago, Carolina had forgotten to tighten up the cinch on Leilani and had been unseated. Kimber had helped her the same way she'd helped Brielle. Carolina hadn't been afraid that any physical harm would come to Brielle, but she didn't want her to lose her confidence and be afraid of horses. But soon she realized there was no danger of that.

If anything, the little wake-up call had helped Kimber bring up the Five Bs, a set of values that were the core of the Unbridled Dreams program.

They were on the other side of the arena, but the soft breeze carried the words all the way to the picnic table.

By now Carolina knew them by heart. The guiding principles weren't meant only for those brief moments riding a horse but were to serve at all times.

Putting them in practice in her daily life was a little harder, to be honest.

1. Be the boss.
2. Be a good teammate.
3. Be focused.
4. Be responsible.
5. Be present.

After the scare, Brielle was definitely present on the saddle. She was being a good boss with Marigold, letting her do her job without giving her too many instructions at once. But she seemed to need to work on staying focused—working on one goal at a time.

"When can I go on the other gears?" Brielle asked.

Abuela Ceci chuckled.

"It's a good question though," Carolina said defensively.

Vida sent her a grateful look. She'd asked the same question during her first lesson.

"The different speeds—walk, trot, canter or lope, and gallop—are called gaits," Kimber explained patiently. "You will learn them soon enough. But first things first. Babies crawl, and then they walk."

"Well . . . when Brielle was a baby, she went straight from sitting to standing and walking. By the time I recovered from the surprise, she was running," Mrs. Stuart whispered behind her hand.

Brielle glanced at her mom. She didn't seem to like being compared to a baby. "Makes sense," she said. "So now we go trotting?"

"Posting the trot is the last skill in the beginner's program," Kimber said.

Brielle's shoulders fell. "Really? I want to take her on a gallop."

"I know how she feels," Chelsie and Carolina said, and then added, "Jinx!"

"Twelve weeks just walking will be boring," Brielle said. "I'm sure I can learn all the gaits in that time."

She sounded so optimistic! But there was a lot to learn while walking on a horse.

Kimber had already given Carolina and Chelsie this lesson when she'd explained that during flat work (that is, when the horse only walks and it looks like the rider isn't doing that much), in reality, there are a lot of wonderful things happening that the untrained eye would not catch: harmony, confidence, and communication.

"Learning the basics takes time. Getting to a gallop as quickly as possible shouldn't be our goal. Don't be hard on yourself if it takes a little longer than you think. Progress isn't a straight line. There can be ups and downs. I want you to get used to riding different horses and styles. Next time you will ride on Napoleon, and then you might try the other horses. This is Western style, but you might prefer English. That's Chelsie's specialty. She's a joy to watch."

Carolina and Vida turned to Chelsie who was now glowing like a neon pink sign.

"A joy to watch indeed!" Caro teased her friend in a mock English accent.

Chelsie smiled at her. The warmth of her gratitude was almost enough to quiet the little jealous part of Caro who was waiting for Kimber to say that Western was Carolina's specialty. But the conversation moved on.

"What if I try hard enough? I can be focused. Hyperfocused! Ask my mom!"

Kimber laughed. "We'll see."

The class continued as Kimber taught Brielle how to make turns and stops, using word commands but most importantly body language and thoughts.

"It's so much to remember!" Brielle said as Kimber led her to the gate.

"One day you'll be able to do everything automatically."

"It's like driving. Only with another sentient being," Brielle said, dismounting.

"That's right," Kimber said.

"I'll write all these goals in my journal. When it's time for the Paradise end-of-summer parade, I'll be ready to post the trot! I promise!"

"I love her gumption!" Carolina said.

Vida just nodded as they walked to congratulate Brielle on her first lesson. The practical part on the horse, that is. They still had to help Marigold cool down.

The two previous Unbridled Dreams students, Gisella and Rockwell, had rushed home at the end of their lessons for different reasons. Carolina was bracing herself to be disappointed, but there was no need for that. Brielle was looking forward to going into the little barn, the best part of the ranch where all Caro's favorite horses lived.

Except for Shadow . . .

Shadow was an exception. He boarded at the ranch because his owners lived in California. But in exchange for feeding and boarding, they allowed him to be a lesson horse.

He now was standing in the shade in the pasture, chewing on grass like he hadn't eaten his feed in the morning. Maybe he just wanted to get his fill of fresh, tender, green grass while it was available, before the scorching sun left it dry and coarse. During the rest of the year, the horses had to make do with eating hay.

After Kimber and Mrs. Stuart headed to the office so she could wait for Brielle in the air-conditioning, Abuela Ceci said, "I'm going to finish making lunch, girls."

"What are you making?" Carolina asked, winking at Chelsie.

"Food, Carola," Abuela Ceci replied, with a smirk on her face.

"What kind?"

"For humans."

"Yay!" Carolina jumped with her fist up. "That's my favorite!"

They all laughed, even Brielle who looked at them going back and forth, unaware that they had the same interaction at least three times a day, for every meal, and sometimes even for snacks.

"See you later, girls," Abuela Ceci said, but then she remembered something and added, "Remember we have our embroidery lesson today."

"I can't wait!" Vida said.

"Yay!" Chelsie cheered.

Carolina winced. Good thing no one seemed to see her reaction.

Crafts weren't her favorite. Yesterday, Abuela Ceci had promised Vida, Carolina, and Chelsie that she'd teach them how to embroider. Carolina hated needles of all kinds. She was only looking forward to the snacks and stories Abuela told them while they avoided the scorching hot afternoon.

Brielle had a look like she wanted to stay too. Carolina's heart swelled like the sky. Gone were the days of being a lonely kid at the ranch. For the first time, she had a group of friends who all loved horses as much as she did—well, almost.

5

Band of Equines

The girls were all dusty and sweaty. And so was Marigold.

"That's a workout!" Brielle said. "I always wondered how horseback riding could be a sport when it seems like the horse does all the work, but . . ." She flexed her arms. "My arms are achy! And my stomach and my legs!"

Carolina smiled, remembering how Rockwell had said the same thing, almost word for word, after his first class.

Vida said, "The horse does most of the work, but the jockey—"

"She means the rider," Carolina cut in.

"Yes, the rider still works hard."

They were almost at the little barn, and Carolina wished they'd taken out the wheelbarrow full of soiled bedding so Brielle wouldn't have a bad first impression.

Too late for that.

But then, as soon as they walked in, Carolina noticed the little barn smelled like pine cleaner.

Judging by the pail of lime back in its spot, Jaime had been around to finish the chores.

Carolina was relieved. Vida looked crestfallen though.

"What's wrong?" Chelsie asked.

"It's just that I wanted to complete my volunteer hour before lunch so I could go to Abuela Ceci's craft lesson."

"You can still do it," Caro said, thinking fast. "Help us cool down Marigold. The more help we get, the faster we'll finish. That counts as volunteering."

"Okay," Vida said.

Brielle stood by the poster with the Five Bs, moving her lips as she read in silence.

Carolina handed her a bottle of cold water and Brielle gulped it down in seconds.

Chelsie put on her favorite Velvet Lilly CD, and the girls started untacking Marigold while Brielle watched their every move.

"Oh my gosh," Brielle said with a gasp, caressing the mare's nose. "I read in books that their noses are soft, but I never imagined . . . This is what heaven must feel like."

"Horse-girl heaven at least," Chelsie said.

There wasn't much room in the stall for a horse and four girls, so Carolina stood aside, happy to let Brielle and Vida take over. She was so happy about how busy and full her little barn felt.

"She's so sweaty!" Brielle said, gently patting the top of Marigold's back. It was darker than the rest of her body from all the sweat.

"Our mountain princess," Chelsie whispered in Marigold's ear as she took the bridle off. "You did so well today. But before you go out with your friends, let's get you nice and cool."

"I'll put that away!" Brielle said. "Where does it go?"

"In the tack room," Carolina pointed. "It's more of a corner than a room, actually. You can find the spot for her bridle there. It has her name on a little plaque."

Brielle wiped the bridle with a clean rag and put it away where it belonged. When she returned to the girls, Vida made room and showed her how to brush the dust off Marigold's coat.

Finally, with kissing sounds, Vida led Marigold outside to the hose.

"Let's only hose down her back and legs," Carolina said, squinting against the bright sun.

"Do horses get sick if they're too hot and should you bathe them with cold water?" Brielle asked.

"Excellent questions," Chelsie said, and turned toward Carolina.

Carolina smiled. It was super nice to see Chelsie in teacher mode. Resisting the urge to take over, she signaled for Chelsie to explain.

"That's only a myth," Chelsie said. "They don't get sick if they're hot and get wet. Actually, if you fail to cool them down, there are so many things that could go wrong. Horses can overheat if it's too hot and humid. Usually, seventeen minutes of exercise is enough to raise their body temperature, and she's been working since this morning."

"Wow!" Brielle said, looking at Chelsie with stars in her eyes. "You know a lot about horses!"

Carolina tried to push down her jealousy one more time.

She was famous for her knowledge of horses, but this wasn't a competition.

"Actually, I did a report for school last year too and I remember all the facts. That's all." Chelsie blushed modestly while she rearranged Marigold's forelock. "Now you're stylish again," she said.

The musky scent of wet horsehair enveloped them for a few seconds, and then the breeze blew it away—carrying the scent of food cooking in the cottage.

"Does she go back to the barn?" Brielle asked, looking back to the little barn as if it were a magical place. Which it was.

"Not until the evening," Chelsie said. "Now she gets to go out with her friends in the pasture."

"Can I meet them too?" Brielle asked.

Carolina and Chelsie beamed at each other again. It was obvious Brielle didn't want to leave the ranch, which was exactly what they wanted the most.

"While you do that," Vida said, "I'll go see if Abuela Ceci needs help with lunch. See you later, Brielle!"

"Bye!" Brielle said.

Mrs. Stuart was patiently waiting in her car, but they promised her they wouldn't take long.

The three girls headed to the pasture where the horses had split into their little friend groups, just like people do. As always, the first one to come welcome them at the gate was Twinkletoes, the mini donkey.

"He's the unofficial welcomer of the band of *equines*," Carolina said, hoping it wasn't obvious she was showing off her knowledge of horses and vocabulary about them. "Twinkletoes, say hi to Brielle."

"I'm going to collapse from the cuteness overload," Brielle said, her hands cupping her mouth as if she didn't want to scare the girls or the horses with loud exclamations. Brielle got on her knees, and hugged Twinks. "He's a real-life Eeyore. Do you know how lucky you are?"

Carolina looked up and gazed at the pasture, the horses making their way to say hi to them, her dog, Boo, sleeping under a tree by the office, the mountains, the wind, the cicadas even.

She nodded.

"Yes," Chelsie said. "We do."

Brielle said hi to every horse, but when she saw Napoleon, the tallest and most intimidating of all, she stepped back and said, "Whoa."

"Don't worry about his size. He's a piece of bread," Carolina said.

Brielle looked at her quizzically.

"She means he's harmless," Chelsie translated. "One of Abuela Ceci's expressions."

Mrs. Stuart honked the horn. "We need to go, Bri!"

Brielle groaned. "Why does time fly when you're having fun?"

It seemed her mom was going to have to drag her from Paradise!

"You can stay to hang out," Carolina offered tentatively. The class was over, but that didn't mean Brielle had to go home yet.

"Thank you." Brielle shook her head. "But my brother has swim team, and then it will be hard for my mom to drive back to get me." Then her face lit up. "Wait! Why don't you all come to the rec center with me! They inaugurated the new pool on Memorial Day, and I've never seen either one of you there."

For weeks, Carolina had been trying to go to the pool, but there had never been an opportunity. Until now.

It's just that town was so far sometimes it felt like it was in another world! Usually, her family planned their visits to check off as many items on the to-do list as possible.

"What day's today?" she asked, chewing on the tip of her thumb.

She could feel the thorn there! If only she could pluck it out!

"Today's Thursday!" Chelsie exclaimed, shaking her head and laughing.

"Right!" Carolina said, trying to visualize the schedule.

No one from Paradise would be in town until the following day. Her mom usually spent Fridays running errands in preparation for the weekend: grocery shopping, runs to the bank, doctor appointments, stopping by the library to restock on books for story time . . .

"Maybe if my mom switches things around . . ." she said, thinking aloud. "Or she could come get me tomorrow?"

"Yes, you can stay at my house! Pajama party!" Brielle said, jumping in the air.

A sleepover! Could Carolina be gone from the barn for so

many hours? Jaime and Tyler could do the barn chores, but what about story time? What about their morning trail ride tomorrow? What about Vida? Would she be okay with the change of plans if they left crafting for another day?

There were so many moving parts . . . but Carolina didn't want this good moment with Brielle to end.

"That would be amazing!" she said. "I have to make sure first though." Her eyes flitted to the cottage where her mom was working, and her heart sank. Her parents had strict rules about sleepovers, meaning, unless the sleepover was at Vida's, they wouldn't give her permission. But maybe, just *maybe* . . . "Should we ask my mom or your mom first, Chels?"

But Chelsie was already shaking her head before Carolina was done asking. "Sorry," she said, "I promised Abuela Ceci I was doing embroidery with her today. Remember we already had plans?"

She looked at Carolina as if begging her to read her mind.

Carolina exhaled, her shoulders falling. "That's right . . ."

In her mind, she tried to find a solution. She wanted everyone to be happy, but the truth was, there was only one option.

But before Carolina could speak, Brielle said, "What about

we plan on going to the pool sometime after my class, instead? Would that make things easier?"

"Much better!" Chelsie said.

Carolina sighed, relieved. "Sure thing!"

"Okay, I'll plan on it!" Brielle said. "See you soon!"

She ran out to the car where her mom was waiting.

Carolina hoped they could all have as much fun at the pool as Brielle had had at her first lesson.

6

That's Fixable

Once Brielle was gone, Carolina and Chelsie trudged up the hill. The sun perched in the top of the sky, directly over their heads. A tiny dust devil swirled in the middle of the graveled path, reminding them that although a lush forest surrounded them, this area was technically part of the Great Basin Desert.

Carolina knew her home state of Idaho was best known for its wild, untamed beauty. Ever since she was little, while her dad fished in the creek that ran by the southern border of the property, Carolina swam in the cool water and pretended she was a seahorse. There even was a small waterfall that she loved. It wasn't impressive like Shoshone Falls in Twin Falls, the "Niagara of the West," but it was still beautiful. She hadn't even had a chance to introduce Chelsie to it, so hectic had their first days of summer been.

Ah! The pool today would have been an oasis!

"I wish we had known about the pool earlier," Carolina said.

Chelsie grimaced. "I don't."

"Why not?"

"I don't like going to the pool. Sorry . . ."

"But why?" Carolina asked, taking her hat off, appalled at the prospect of never going to the pool with Chelsie. Swimming was at the top of her summer to-do list, and it wouldn't be the same without Chelsie.

Today had been a rare summer day that Chelsie had been home all day. Her calendar was full of all the dressage competitions she and Velvet had signed up for months ago. Next year, Chelsie and Velvet would move on to eventing, which was like a triathlon consisting of dressage, cross-country, and show jumping.

Carolina was happy for her friend, but it meant they wouldn't have time for all the summer fun Caro wanted to share with her. They lived on the same property, and they still couldn't find time for everything! What if their different interests pulled them further and further apart? Carolina's shoulders slumped.

"I don't know how to swim," Chelsie admitted.

Carolina laughed, relieved. "Chels! That's fixable! I can teach you!"

"You?"

"Yes! Finally, I can return the favor for helping me with the dance."

At the end of the school year, Vida and Chelsie had helped Carolina get her two left feet in line. If it weren't for them, she never would've been ready for the sixth-grade dance. She wasn't going to get any awards for being the most graceful dancer, but they'd helped her have fun.

"We'll see," Chelsie said.

"But what is it? Are you scared of the water?"

Instead of replying, Chelsie sent her a pleading look.

Carolina got the message.

Curiosity vibrated through her from head to toe, but she wouldn't pester her friend. In fact, she'd learned from experience that the more she pressured Chelsie to share something, the less Chelsie wanted to open up to her.

Perhaps during their nightly chats at Velvet's stall, the topic would come back up.

When Chelsie and Carolina walked in, Vida was just finishing setting the table for lunch while Abuela Ceci brought over a tray lined with carne asada tortas.

"My favorite!" Carolina said, rushing to help her grandma.

Abuela clicked her tongue. "Wash your hands first."

Chelsie was already drying hers.

"Vida arrived at the perfect time to help me assemble the sandwiches," Abuela said.

Vida beamed. "I'm glad I could help and learn! These are my favorite sandwiches too."

Carolina started on the delicious, rich food happily. Then, she shared the idea she'd gotten watching Vida record Brielle's lesson: Maybe they could take pictures and video throughout the program, to present to the student as a parting gift.

"I just wish we had thought about this last year! Too bad we can't turn back time," she said with a sigh.

"At least we can do it for Brielle," Vida said.

Carolina loved how she said "we," like she truly felt part of Paradise too. Their program was finally really taking off.

But if they didn't get more support from the community, Unbridled Dreams might end before they could put all their brilliant ideas into practice.

"Ready for embroidering?" Abuela Ceci asked.

"Yes!" Vida and Chelsie exclaimed.

Carolina started cleaning up the table while her friends went through Abuela's thread collection in every color of the rainbow. Since there was no point in trying to embroider since she couldn't even thread a needle, Carolina spent the whole time just picking at the thorn in her finger. But all she accomplished was pushing it deeper into her skin.

By the end of the day, after evening chores, and dinner, her mom insisted she take a look at it. "I think we'll have to get the doctor to take this out."

"Why?" Carolina asked, tucking her hand in the pockets of her pajama pants.

"It's pushed too far into the fleshy part of your thumb. If you'd rather not have the doctor pluck it out, we might be able to wait until your body expels it naturally."

"I'll wait," Carolina replied.

Over the next few days, the poke in her hand healed—sort

of. Skin grew over it like a zit that didn't hurt, but Carolina hated it. She tried to ignore it, but being in the center of her thumb pad, it bothered her. From then on, every time they went on their morning trail ride, she made sure she wore riding gloves. She didn't want to end up covered in infected prickles.

The apple branches kept spreading over the deer trail until they tangled with the trees on the other side and formed a perfect arch.

Every time they rode past it, Carolina ducked, and her hand throbbed as if to remind her that the thorn was still there. Or maybe it was her imagination.

7

Trying to Speak Horse

A few days later, Vida was excited for her next lesson with Napoleon. Although he was the tallest and biggest horse in the ranch, he was one of the kindest, most patient ones. A perfect teacher.

With Carolina hovering around her like a worried mother hen, Vida groomed and tacked him all on her own. She struggled to place the saddle because it was so heavy and Napoleon was so tall, but she finally did it all by herself.

"Ta-da!" she exclaimed, with such a look of pride on her face, Carolina couldn't help but cheer.

"Brava!"

Napoleon's ears twitched, but Carolina was too happy to be offended by his silent reminder to keep her voice down inside the stable. Especially now that Vida was carefully, slowly, but correctly cinching him up.

Shadow had been—not so patiently—waiting in his own stall, all ready to go, for several minutes. He snorted so loudly that Vida flinched.

"It's just Shadow," Carolina reassured her, and Vida continued threading the long leather cinch until it was tight enough.

Vida had always been hesitant when it came to the horses. Carolina had never understood why she was so afraid of them—until a few months ago when Vida shared with Gisella that she'd had a scary experience that had put her off horses. During a carnival pony ride, a horse had chewed on her pigtails. As the years went by, the fear increased to an irrational level.

Helping Carolina do chores had decreased the fear again, until she got the courage to take lessons so she could join her friends on lazy trail rides.

But it also meant that with Vida, they had to go at a slower pace than usual. By the time she was done tacking the horse and completed the join up, there wasn't a lot of time for actual riding.

Vida was okay with this, and Kimber was patient. She didn't mind that Vida seemed content to take Napoleon on a slow walk in the outside ring.

Carolina, who had expected to race Vida in the pasture like she did with Chelsie, was a little disappointed. But seeing Vida do the same boring walk around the ring was also oddly calming. Kimber had suggested that instead of sitting to watch the lesson, she took the chance to work with Shadow on mindful walking too. The ring was big enough for both pairs of girl and horse.

Every once in a while, Kimber would break the silence and remind the girls—mainly Caro—that good horsemanship was a repetition of actions. "Seasons provide some variety, but it's all the same kind of work. At the same time, every day and every ride is different. That's the beauty of it. It's a lifelong pursuit. It's a practice, not a race, and everyone goes at their own pace."

She was right, of course.

Last week, Vida had learned how to communicate without word commands. On her third lesson! Something that had taken Carolina years to accomplish and now Vida and Napoleon seemed to share one mind.

Just because her friends learned on a different time line, it didn't mean that it was wrong or worse. Carolina could learn a lot from Vida too.

Following Vida's example, she sat deeper in the saddle and tried to breathe mindfully, that is, intentionally. Her efforts paid off.

Soon, after a loud snort, Shadow's breaths matched hers. His body relaxed. Head hanging, he followed Carolina's lead around the ring.

The wind blew from the mountains, making music in the tree leaves that joined the song of the birds and the distant barking of Boo.

Suddenly, Carolina's attention got snagged by a little detail. Shadow wasn't exactly limping, but his gait was a little stiff. She had to adjust her perch on the saddle to remain balanced.

She winced as if it was her leg throbbing with pain and not the horse's.

"Everything okay, Caro?" Kimber asked from the center of the arena. She might have been quiet, but she was attentive to everything.

"I don't know . . ." Carolina said, wishing she could see

inside Shadow's mind and read his thoughts. Instead, she closed her eyes and tried to hear what he couldn't say with words. After a few seconds, it was obvious. He was limping slightly in both hind legs.

"I hope it's not his hocks acting up again," she whispered.

Kimber was already by her side, and Carolina brought Shadow to a halt just using her leads, tightening her tummy, and squeezing her thighs. He obeyed promptly.

Late last year, he'd been in pain and no one but Carolina had figured out that there was a problem in his hind knees. That experience had taught her to listen and see with her heart for things that were silent and invisible. She was glad she hadn't forgotten the lesson, and neither had he lost his trust in her.

Kimber looked at Carolina. "I think it's his hocks again. Is this the first time you've noticed?"

Now that she thought about it, Carolina realized Shadow had given her plenty of clues. She told Kimber about how hesitant he'd been to walk downhill on the trail and how hard it was for him to break into a gallop lately.

"Maybe he's just tired?" Carolina suggested.

Perhaps this was the first time she'd been connected with Shadow in a while. On rides, she was always chatting or distracted, looking around. This exercise of walking without a specific goal had yielded a lot of surprising results.

"Yes, maybe he's just tired," Kimber said, but there was caution in her voice. "Let's untack him and stable him until Dr. Rooney can take a look at him later."

Carolina clicked her tongue, and Shadow's tail twitched as if he too was frustrated that his old injury had returned.

The vision of climbing up to Sleeping Princess Rock with him vanished.

"Everything okay?" asked Vida.

Kimber gave her a thumbs-up and said to Carolina, "I'll finish with Vida first?"

"Okay," Carolina said. Before dismounting, she leaned forward and whispered in his ear, "Hang in there, Shadow."

They made it back to the barn just as some of the wranglers were moving the boarding horses to the pasture. Abuela Ceci apparently had been passing out aguas frescas because she stood by the barn with an empty pitcher in one hand and a stack of plastic cups in the other.

Seeing Carolina's expression, a cloud crossed her face and blotted her smile. "What's wrong, Carola?"

Carolina's eyes prickled with emotion as she told her grandma the news.

Abuela Ceci listened in silence, and after she put the cups inside the pitcher, she caressed Shadow's mane. He had leaves stuck in it, hitchhikers from their morning ride.

"Do you think he'll be all right?" Carolina asked, anxiously.

Abuela Ceci didn't hesitate. "I'm sure he will be. If it was the hocks that were bothering him a few months ago, maybe this is the same thing. Worrying before we know for sure is pointless. It only makes him nervous. Look how tense he is."

And he was.

"Whatever it is, we'll take care of you, beautiful Shadow," Abuela Ceci whispered in his ear.

"Yes, we will," Carolina promised.

There was a sound of hoofbeats, and Shadow looked up. Marigold was galloping in the pasture, a trail of dust behind her, toward a water trough next to the far fence. She didn't like the automatic one for some reason. With a neigh, she called to her friends. Bella and Leilani galloped toward the water trough as if they'd planned it ahead of time.

Shadow looked toward the pasture with longing. Carolina felt his desire to join his friends too, to gallop free with the wind tangling his mane. But they couldn't let him run until they knew what was wrong with him.

Poor Shadow! He must have wondered why the change in routine. He always joined his friends after a lesson. What must he be thinking now?

Carolina remembered what Michael had told her a few months ago about Napoleon when he wasn't digesting his food right. A change in routine created uncertainty in a horse's life, and uncertainty created stress.

When they'd untacked Shadow, Carolina placed her hands on the sides of his face and pressed her nose to his. They breathed each other's air for a couple of heartbeats. A first. He'd never let her do that before.

"Tonight, Dr. Rooney is going to see you, and everything will be okay, Shadow," she said, hoping her voice gave him confidence. Confidence she didn't really feel but wanted to. "We'll be out on the trail and in the pastures in no time."

The horse snorted, and she wrapped her arms around him. "You're home, Shadow. You're safe."

Home, when it was a physical place, could change. But the things that anchored a person in love remained forever.

Home is where the heart is, and there's no place like it.

She didn't know how to tell him this in words a horse could understand. She didn't know how to express these words even for herself, but she felt them like a warm seed in her heart that spread its roots through her body.

She hoped Shadow felt this.

Now they could only wait to see what the vet said.

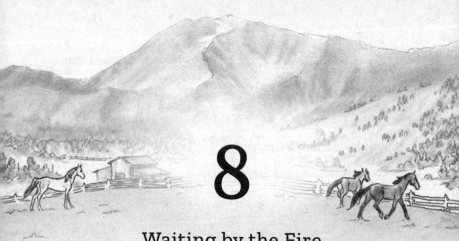

8

Waiting by the Fire

Chelsie and her mom had gone shopping for new riding boots. By the time they returned to the ranch, there was only a faint glow in the sky beyond the mountains. In the cool mansion house, fueled by homemade cherry ice cream, Carolina was filling her friend in on the news. Then the sound of wheels on gravel alerted them that someone had arrived.

"Dr. Rooney!" Chelsie exclaimed.

"Finally!" Carolina added, running to peek out the window.

It was dark, but sure enough, his black pickup truck was parked by the big barn.

"Let's go!" she called, heading to the front door with Chelsie one step behind her.

They raced each other to the barn to hear what he had

to say about Shadow. But Tyler stopped them in the doorway. "Ms. Whitby asked me to keep you entertained until Dr. Rooney is done with his rounds."

"His rounds?" Chelsie asked, alarmed. "Who else is he seeing?"

Tyler's face reddened as he ruffled his curly hair. "Sorry, Chels. I can't say that either. Wait until she and Amado are done, and they'll tell you themselves."

Asking the girls, especially Carolina, to wait after waiting all day long was like asking a fire not to burn. Or the sun not to rise in the morning.

When Caro opened her mouth to argue, he put a hand up as if he still hoped to stop an avalanche from running downhill. "Believe me, I want to know too. Shadow was my first horse."

"Oh, Tyler," Chelsie said, patting his arm.

The silence pounded in Carolina's ears, but, miracle of miracles, she couldn't speak or move. The love for Shadow in Tyler's voice disarmed her. Ever since Tyler had left for college, one thing after another had happened to Shadow. She should've taken better care of him.

"I'm sorry." Her eyes welled with tears, and Tyler panicked.

"No need for sad faces! Shadow has been through worse. Like . . . remember when we went riding in the old pastures beyond the orchard and he got a nasty gash from some barbed wire I didn't see?"

"Yikes!" Chelsie exclaimed, her hands flying to her eyes as if she was trying to block a vision.

Carolina had tried hard to bury the memory of calming Shadow while Dr. Rooney stitched him up. Now it resurfaced and made her shiver.

Seeing that his words were making things worse, Tyler looked desperately around for something that would cheer the girls up. He didn't have to look far.

"We're singing by the fire," he said, pointing toward the firepit. "We have s'mores and other treats!"

Carolina and Chelsie exchanged a look. More than the treats, it was the proximity of the firepit to the barn that convinced them. Their parents wouldn't be able to sneak out of the office without giving them an update.

Chelsie gestured with her head for Carolina to follow her. "Let's go," she said.

Carolina glanced back at the stables. What was going on, and was there anything they could do?

"We'll let you choose the song," Tyler said.

"Okay," Carolina finally said, hooking her arm in the crook of his elbow like old times. And then she hooked the other in Chelsie's so her friend wouldn't feel left out.

Even in the peak of summer, nights at Paradise were cool. The crackling fire was soothing and inviting. Especially with the s'mores that JC and Andrew, two of the wranglers who'd been there as long as Caro could remember, were already assembling.

The ranchers were all part of the family, and it was a summer tradition to gather for a short time to end the day together. Although Carolina loved it so much, this was the first time she'd joined the ranch hands at the firepit this summer, and she regretted not introducing Chelsie to this tradition until now. Although they were waiting for possibly troubling news, sitting under the stars while Andrew strummed the guitar was comforting. In any case, it was better than waiting alone, pacing in her room.

"What's the first song, Carolina?" JC asked, teasing her by

pronouncing her name Caro-lie-na, like the state.

He succeeded in making her smile, but she could tease him too.

She pretended to think, tapping her index finger on her chin, but they all knew what she was going to say. She always chose the same song.

"'Clementine!'" she finally exclaimed.

They all laughed, even Chelsie. Andrew started plucking his guitar. His style was a little rustic, but there was a sense of joy in the way he played and in the twang of his voice.

Once they'd run out of lyrics, they continued another tradition: making up funny lines that got more and more ludicrous as they ran out of rhyming words.

"Oh my darling, Clementine!" Carolina and Chelsie were singing the chorus at the top of their lungs when the sound of an engine coming to life cut their words short.

Their voices stopped like someone had muted them.

It was the vet, and he was gone before the girls snapped out of their surprise.

"Dr. Rooney didn't look so happy," Carolina whispered, fear rooting her in place.

"He didn't," Chelsie added.

"Everything will be all right," Tyler said, always an optimist. "You'll see."

Carolina didn't know if his words were more for himself or for the girls. It didn't matter—she was ready to bolt and demand some answers.

In that moment, Heather walked out of the office, and looking toward the campfire, she called, "Chelsie! Caro! Come over here!"

Without wasting a second, they raced toward Heather. Tyler followed them, but Andrew and JC stayed by the fire.

Carolina tried to leave all her fears behind, but they clung to her like burrs. Tyler headed to Shadow's stall, but Carolina's dad stopped the girls and ushered them into the office instead.

"This can't be good," Carolina whispered, but then she realized that Heather was smiling.

Chelsie's mom was usually reserved and cautious, like her daughter. But now her eyes were twinkling.

"Guess what?"

"What?" Chelsie asked while Caro looked at her dad for

clues. He was smiling too, but there was a cloud of worry in his eyes.

"In a couple of months, we'll have a newborn horse at Paradise!" Heather exclaimed, her hands clasped in front of her as if she was trying not to clap with excitement.

This was such different news from what they were expecting that the girls didn't know how to react.

"What? How?" Chelsie asked.

"Is Shadow having a baby?" Carolina asked, although she knew this was impossible. But she succeeded in getting some laughter out of her dad and Ms. Whitby and in calming herself. At least a little.

"Oh, Carolina!" Heather said, laughing.

"Tell us quickly before we collapse!" Chelsie said, for once losing her patience.

Amado chuckled and shook his head. "You horse-crazy girls!"

Caro sat next to her dad, and Chelsie sat on the desk. Kimber always kept it in order so there was no danger of misplacing important papers.

"Yesterday, I received a call from a horse rescue operation,"

Heather said. "They have a pregnant mare, and they don't have the space for her—or her baby once it arrives. They asked if I'd be willing to take them—"

"You said yes, of course!" Chelsie cut in.

A mama and her foal! Of course they had plenty of room!

"Dibs on naming the baby!" Carolina called, raising a hand like she was at school.

Immediately, Chelsie shook her head and exclaimed, "Absolutely not! I'll name it!"

"Girls, listen, please!" Amado Aguasvivas said, and the plea in his soft voice was enough to quiet them down.

Heather sent him a grateful look and continued, "There were so many things to consider, Chels. But after analyzing numbers and costs, and talking with Jen and Amado, we all decided that yes, we can afford to take them in."

"But they're from a rescue so they're for free, right?" Chelsie asked.

"There's no such thing as free," Carolina reminded her. "Especially when it comes to animals."

"True that," Papi said. "When you take them in, you must consider the expenses of keeping them fed and healthy, and plan for unexpected expenses of every kind. As you both know, something always comes up."

"Like this thing with Shadow," Heather said, exhaling.

Just like that, the excitement over a newborn horse left the room like air from a popped balloon.

What was wrong with Shadow?

Carolina saw Tyler standing by the office door to hear the news. They exchanged a look that meant that whatever happened, they'd get through this together.

Shadow might not be the "horse of her heart," but Carolina loved him unconditionally.

"Shadow's getting on in years, and his hocks have been bothering him for a while. Last time, the treatment only helped for a little while," Papi said, looking Caro straight in the eyes. The words were honest, but they still hurt. She didn't like to think that the horses were getting old, but at least she knew her dad wasn't leaving details out to spare her. "His arthritis is much worse than anything Dr. Rooney has seen in a while."

Tyler clicked his tongue.

"Arthritis?" Carolina asked, placing her hands over her racing heart.

"Aunt Bernice had arthritis in her hands," Chelsie said, her face the image of worry. "It's very painful. She had surgery for it, right, Mama?"

"Right," said Ms. Whitby.

"Will Shadow need surgery?" Chelsie asked.

Carolina was grateful that her friend was collected enough to ask the important questions.

"Dr. Rooney is still trying to decide. He suggested a treatment and a change in diet, but if that doesn't work, then laser surgery is an option to fuse his bones. Usually after the bones are fused, pain decreases considerably."

"It's so expensive though," Tyler said. He was studying to be a vet one day. Although he was still taking his general classes, he worked part-time at a vet clinic in Boise.

"We've traded for services with Dr. Rooney in the past, right?" Carolina said. "He can give us a discount if he treats him at his office?" She tightened a fist in her sweatshirt pocket. Now her face burned and not because of the campfire. She was already thinking of volunteering to answer phones or clean the kennels in his clinic, training his horses, anything that would help with the cost.

Anything for Shadow.

"Dr. Rooney doesn't have the right equipment in his office. Shadow would have to be transported to Boise," Heather explained.

Carolina's heart hammered so hard that when she spoke, her voice was shaky. "His owners, the ones in California, need to take care of his health, though, right? That's what a responsible owner does."

She looked around for support. Chelsie nodded, but Heather, whose cheeks were bright red, looked at Caro's dad.

"We've been talking with his owners about this since he had problems with his hocks last time. They said that they were considering selling Shadow in the auction at the end of the summer. Transporting him and paying for surgery might be too big an expense they don't want to assume."

His words flew around Caro's mind like vultures picking at roadkill.

She had never met Shadow's owners. They'd been friends with Mr. Parry, and when they moved, Shadow had stayed behind. They didn't love him the way everyone at Paradise did. How would he start all over somewhere new? How could there be a Paradise without their gray angel?

"He's almost twelve, like us," Carolina said, looking at Chelsie.

That was getting on in years for a horse, though not terribly old. But Shadow's previous life as a jumper had taken a toll on him.

The girls held each other's anguished gaze.

"Can't we buy him from them?" Chelsie asked, turning toward her mom. "Being an Arabian, and with his champion history, I know he might cost a lot."

"That's not the issue," Heather said. "His owners are willing to let him go for almost nothing. But the surgery . . ."

"We must have funds for emergencies," Chelsie said. "There has to be a way to pay for it."

Heather sighed deeply. "If only I knew this would happen before we gave our word to take in this mare, sweetheart . . . It's such bad timing."

Carolina really wanted to tell them that Shadow had priority. But if Heather and her dad had given their word, then, there was no way to go back on it.

She'd never felt more helpless. How she wished she could wave a magic wand and cure Shadow or, at least, find a pot of gold at the end of the rainbow to make sure he wasn't in pain.

"I thought . . ." Carolina said, her voice hoarse. "I was hoping to ride on him for the end-of-summer parade." Which was really one of the last and least reasons she had to save Shadow, but it was the first she blurted out.

"Oh, Caro," her dad said, and hugged her.

She hid her face in his shoulder, trying not to let the tears fall.

Judging by the sniffling coming from the other corner of the office, Chelsie was crying. Tyler had left quietly, most likely back to Shadow's stall.

Caro wasn't the only one struggling with the news.

"We'll try our best to get him the care he needs, and if he has to leave us, we'll make sure he goes where he'll be loved and protected," Caro's dad said.

He didn't need to add that it was a promise. Carolina knew that his words were unbreakable.

9

Smells Like Summer

Although Carolina was trying to savor each minute of sweet summer, the news of Shadow's health had definitely left a bitter taste in her mouth. She hated needles, but when he needed a shot of anti-inflammatory medicine, she was right next to him trying to offer comfort and strength.

Over the next several days, Caro, Vida, and Chelsie took turns hand-walking Shadow, massaging his legs, and making sure he stuck to the strict diet Dr. Rooney had suggested. But then Chelsie left for a horse show in Boise, and Vida had cheer camp. She wanted to audition for the eighth-grade cheer squad in August and had to perfect her roundoff backspring tuck, whatever that was.

All the tasks fell on Carolina.

To say the Arabian wasn't happy was an understatement. Trail rides were out of the question. Until his pain subsided, Shadow wasn't allowed to run in the pasture either. He spent the afternoons standing in the middle of his solitary little paddock, gazing at his friends with longing.

Bracken, Carolina's little assistant, rounded up help from Gisella and a few other kids. They brought a pile of books to read to the Arabian, but Shadow ignored them, so most of them went to pet Twinks, Bella, and Boo instead.

By the time it was Friday morning, Carolina was ready for a break. After Brielle's class, they were heading to the community center for some time at the pool.

"How did class go?" Mrs. Stuart asked as they drove to town.

Brielle's face lit up. "It was a blast! I think Napoleon is my favorite. I'm in love with him!"

A sweet glow like warm honey spread through Carolina's chest. Napoleon had been Rockwell's favorite horse too, not only to ride, but to talk to and tell all his secrets. She and Rockwell still messaged occasionally, and Carolina was happy he and his brother, Bronco, continued riding horses with a program in Chicago. She wished he hadn't moved so far.

"He's a tall horse!" Mrs. Stuart said. "It's a long way to fall from that saddle."

"At least I have a good-fitting helmet now," Brielle said. "Kimber said she got it thinking of me."

"What do you mean?" Carolina asked. She'd noticed a new blue one in the main tack room, but she'd thought one of the boarders might have left it on accident.

"The other day, the helmet didn't really fit because of my hair," Brielle said. "Kimber noticed that the strap was low-key choking me, and she wanted me to be nice and comfy." She shrugged, but her eyes were shiny.

"I'm sorry!" Carolina said, appalled she hadn't noticed. "You should've told me."

"I didn't know it wasn't supposed to be like that! I still don't know so many things! Kimber said she can usually make do by braiding her hair flat, but when it's natural like mine, she has a hard time finding one that works."

Carolina was so glad Kimber had noticed that none of their existing helmets were a good fit for Brielle! This was proof that the more people they worked with, the more they learned. Although her hair was long and thick, Carolina never had to worry about her helmet fitting. She had never realized how this wouldn't be the same experience for everyone else. Now they knew for the future.

That is, if there was still a future for Unbridled Dreams. She wanted to hold on to hope that they would get more funding for their program, but with Shadow's health problems added in the mix, there were a lot of obstacles in their way.

So many thoughts crowded in her mind and the drive to town was long. A dangerous combination. At least the views were beautiful. Carolina never tired of gazing at the bright blue sky, the snowcapped mountains, and the emerald green grass. During a lull in the conversation, Mrs. Stuart put some music on.

Carolina had learned to love the K-pop tunes of Velvet Lilly that Vida and Chelsie (and every kid in their grade) were obsessed with. But left to her own devices, she gravitated to old people's music, as she called the songs her dad loved: '80s and '90s, with the occasional 2000s thrown in.

As the car glided down the country road, the three of them listened in appreciation to "9 to 5," a Dolly Parton bop that came on in Carolina's house all the time. Carolina smiled when Mrs. Stuart and Brielle took turns singing their favorite parts. And she breathed in relief that neither turned around for her to join them. She only sang in the shower and sometimes with the animals.

As they neared Paradise, Carolina watched an endless parade of *For Sale* signs flash by marking orchards, farms, and ranches.

She reminded herself of what her mom had told her on their last drive: It wasn't a tragedy that the land was being sold.

After all, the best thing that had happened to Paradise Ranch was the arrival of a new owner in Heather who had a great vision of what the property could become. What made Carolina sad were the signs advertising new housing developments. The fields and pastures that made Paradise into a dream town would be divided up and made into neighborhoods.

She couldn't resent the newcomers. After all, every person who wasn't Indigenous like Michael had moved here from somewhere, including the pioneers and settlers, even Carolina's family. Throughout history, people migrated from place to place. It was a part of life.

She couldn't resent the families who had sold the land

either. Ranchers who had been in the area for generations were forced to leave because they weren't making money, or their children moved away. Or the price offered for their land was just too high to reject. She knew only too well that life on a ranch is a life of sacrifice.

Still, it was sad to see that one of the oldest apple orchards was gone forever, replaced by rows and rows of modern houses, white vinyl fences crisscrossing what not even two years ago had been pastureland.

If all the farms were gone, then what would people eat?

"Hand me my backpack, please?" Brielle asked, looking over her shoulder to Carolina. "My feet are killing me."

Carolina shook off her spiraling thoughts. Like Brielle, she was still wearing her riding clothes. She was so hot she wouldn't be surprised if her feet had melted inside her boots.

"We should've changed back at the ranch!" she exclaimed.

"No problem," said Brielle, yanking off a boot. "They have super nice lockers in the community center."

Quietly, her mom rolled down the window. The scent of sunshine and grass quickly blew away the smell of stinky feet. Carolina had a pair of flip-flops Vida had given her for her birthday last year, but she was too self-conscious to even attempt to take off her boots in the car too. Plus, she was nervous about what she'd brought to change into.

Living far from town, being an only child, without a phone, sometimes she felt so out of the loop on what was cool!

She should've asked Vida, but she hadn't thought of it until it was too late to call. The night before, trying not to second-guess herself, she had packed a mesh string backpack for the pool. She picked a white sundress, one of the only things in her closet that wasn't jeans and witty T-shirts. It was a few years old. Abuela Ceci had said it was perfect as a cover-up, but now Carolina wondered if she should've just brought shorts and a long T-shirt.

But worse was the one-piece yellow swimsuit her mom had bought her the last time they'd gone shopping.

Just when her thoughts were starting to send her into a new downward spiral, her nose detected the scent of chlorine. The sounds of happy children and splashing water made her smile and drove her nerves away.

"Finally!" Brielle exclaimed, ready to jump out of the car the instant her mom parked it. She ran toward the entrance where there was a short line of people waiting to go in.

"Go ahead, Carolina," Mrs. Stuart said as she stretched a silver sunshade inside the windshield. "I'll be right behind you."

When she was little, Carolina used to come to the rec center all the time for swimming lessons. But the whole place had been remodeled the year before. Now she felt a bout of shyness as she headed toward Brielle.

But she didn't need to worry. The nice elderly lady at the front table checked Brielle's ID with a big smile and welcomed Caro in as a guest. They both got smeared horse stamps on their hands.

"It must be a sign!" Brielle said.

"The best sign!"

It was hard not to smile with such a welcome and the lovely view in front of her past the main gate. The blue pool glittered under the sun. Dozens of kids lined up in front of tall slides in primary colors for three seconds of adrenaline as they barreled down into the water.

Last year, Carolina hadn't come to the pool because Vida

was in the Philippines and Chelsie hadn't moved to the ranch yet. She didn't want to cross paths with Tessa and Loretta and be at the pool all by herself.

But with a friend, things were different. Even if technically she'd just met Brielle, they had clicked.

"Hi, Mom!" A little Black boy of around seven years old called from the pool. He was surrounded by a few other boys his age and a teacher who was trying to lead them away from the deep end without success. It looked like herding the horses when they didn't want to leave the pasture at night.

"Hi, baby!" Mrs. Stuart called from behind them.

When she waved, the bangles on her wrist tinkled like bells.

The boy ducked at the sound of the endearment, and the other boys teased him.

Squinting her eyes against the glare of the sun on the water, Carolina asked, "Is that your brother?"

Brielle had a smile in her voice when she said, "Yes, that's Jesse. Everywhere we go he's Mr. Popular. I don't know how he does it." Her love for him was loud and clear though. The typical older sister.

From one of the cabanas, a bunch of girls waved at them,

and Brielle waved back. Although Brielle had moved to the area only last winter, she seemed to know *everyone*. Carolina searched the group for Vida, who'd said she might join them, but didn't see her best friend's bright rainbow hair. But she did recognize Gisella Bassi from under a wide-brimmed hat, and waved.

Gisella waved back. She was still shy and reserved, but her confidence had bloomed in the last few months—especially after she'd done the Unbridled Dreams program.

"Let's go change," Brielle said, pulling Carolina by the hand.

"I'll save this lounge chair and umbrella!" Mrs. Stuart said as the girls headed to the lockers.

10

Splash!

The rec center might have looked brand-new and modern, but the lockers and bathrooms smelled the same as ever. Anyone would think that after being at the stables all day every day, smells wouldn't bother Carolina. She had her limits though. And the combination of sweat, mold, and chlorine usually made her stomach roil.

She and Brielle chose side-by-side stalls to change into their swimsuits. Carolina was sweating by the time she managed to pull it all the way up and tie it behind her neck. She wondered what kind of swimsuit Brielle would wear.

The whole time, Brielle chatted like a chipmunk about what she wanted to do this summer. It was nice to find someone who could keep up with Carolina's speed of talking. The problem was finding a gap here and there to give her own opinion of things.

"When we go berry picking, I'll let you know so you can come along. It would be a lot better if you had a phone though," said Brielle. They both walked out of their stalls at the same time. Carolina was relieved to see that her friend's swimsuit was similar to hers—one piece, not a bikini—but in a flowery fabric instead of solid.

Brielle rummaged in her bag, pulled out a tube of sunscreen, and squeezed too much on her hand. "Oops," she said, trying to spread the thick goo down her arms.

"Let me help you," said Carolina. "Then you help me. I don't want to burn the first time at the pool in forever."

In that moment, the door slammed open. It must have been the force of the breeze that added extra *bam!*, but seeing Loretta and Tessa walking in, Carolina wondered why they always had to make an entrance.

A few girls followed them. Some were from school, but most were strangers. Brielle seemed to know them because two of them smiled at her and nodded in greeting.

At first Loretta acted like the locker room was empty, but when she saw Carolina, her eyes narrowed.

"Hey, Loretta," Carolina said, taking the bull by the horns, as Tyler liked to say.

She tried to make her voice sound friendly, but there was so much baggage between the two of them that no matter how she said things, Loretta always took it the wrong way.

But this time, her face softened. "Oh, it's you," she replied. "Hi."

Carolina was caught off guard by the greeting. There was an awkward silence, and then she asked, "Weren't you going to the horse show in Montana with Chelsie?"

Loretta's cheeks reddened, but she inhaled deeply as if she was picking her words carefully. Finally, she said, "Change of plans."

Before Carolina could ask what she meant, Loretta walked into one of the stalls. Her friends shifted in place, like they were bursting to share a secret.

Carolina had known Loretta since they were both little. But a few years ago, Loretta had gone to a fancy summer camp in Boise and came back believing Carolina was less than her, somehow. Since then, they'd grown apart to the point that they had become strangers to each other. Carolina couldn't say she knew her anymore. Her curiosity itched uncomfortably, but she wasn't going to ask and risk being rejected, or worse, become the butt of jokes. That's what usually happened with this group of girls.

Hands full of sunscreen, Carolina caught Brielle's eye and motioned to head outside. They had sunshine to enjoy instead.

· U ·

The pool was way more fun than Carolina had imagined. At least for a while, worries about Shadow, Unbridled Dreams, and Loretta retreated to the back of her mind. She and Brielle chased Jesse and his friends around the lazy river, going opposite the current to make it more challenging—and fun! After that, they went down the slides about fifty times. Then it was jumping from the diving board even though all Carolina could do was the cannonball.

Her swimming lessons had been basic, and she hadn't learned to swim in different strokes or dives.

But it didn't matter.

Her new friend never made fun of her. Brielle didn't seem to care that her swimsuit didn't have a cute print like hers. She felt as free with Brielle's family as if she were galloping on the prairie, spreading her arms wide like in the movie about a castaway boy and a lost horse that her parents liked to watch sometimes.

After so much splashing, running, swimming, jumping, and bonding, Carolina's stomach protested so loudly, Brielle heard it.

"My stomach is eating itself too," Brielle said. "Let's go eat something before I go full-on shark mode."

"You don't want to see shark mode activated," Jesse said, making a gesture like sharks had claws.

After they got burgers and fruit from the concession stand, they sat on towels in a shady area. For a moment, there was only the sounds of chewing and gulping, with splashing and screaming and laughing from the pool behind them.

"Are you going to McAllister Middle School next year?" Brielle asked. She had three different sets of tan lines criss-crossing her shoulders.

"Yes, I'll be at McAllister!" Carolina stretched out on her towel. The prickly grass made her feet tickle.

"What classes are you taking? Maybe we can be together!" Brielle said, lying next to Carolina.

The kids from their valley attended different elementary schools, but they all got together for middle and high school. This meant that the classes were huge, and although they were both taking similar subjects, they might not share any periods.

"Next time I come over for my lesson, I'll bring my schedule printout. What do you think?" Brielle said.

"Sounds like a plan!" Carolina replied, hoping that they'd be together at least for one class. She hadn't thought about this before, and now she worried that Vida and Chelsie would have different schedules. They'd all been so excited to finish sixth grade and hadn't considered that they might not see each other all day long next school year.

What if she ended up sharing classes with Loretta?

Carolina spotted her lounging by the water, a sad expression on her face. Between that and her funny greeting in the locker room, something seemed to be up with her. Carolina was so sick of the tension between them, and of dreading every time she saw her. Was seventh grade going to be the same?

Brielle noticed where Caro's eyes had landed. "She's so . . ." Brielle said, clenching her hands into fists as if she were fighting to find the right word.

"Stuck up?" suggested Carolina.

Brielle pursed her lips and then added, "That's putting it lightly." It sounded like Brielle had had a rocky start with Loretta.

After Caro and Loretta grew apart, Loretta had bullied Carolina and called her Pooper Scooper until Heather had made it mandatory for all students to muck stalls. Loretta had made fun of Caro's friendship with and crush on Rockwell. She was mean to her own little brother, Bracken. And she walked around like she was constantly smelling something rotten.

But . . .

Before she turned so mean, Loretta had been Carolina's best friend. They'd spent so many days playing pretend cowgirls, running around the yard with horse-sticks until they learned how to ride real horses. They'd been inseparable.

Now Carolina had been starting to notice the cruelty behind some of Loretta's comments about people with darker skin, heavier weight, or an untraditional name. As the years went by, she'd become meaner—and sadder.

Carolina might not have liked Loretta, or known what was in her heart, but she didn't enjoy seeing her so upset.

Maybe it was time to mend their fences and make their peace. Start middle school with a clean slate.

The idea perked her up. She didn't know how to change things between them after so long . . . but if it had changed once, maybe it could again, right?

She felt Brielle's gaze on her, waiting for Caro to agree, and didn't want to sound like she was trying to be better than her or anything. Carolina just shrugged, thoughtful.

In that moment, she had the distinct feeling that someone was watching her, and she turned and locked eyes with Tessa, who stood at the concession stand, two ice-cream cones in her hands. Obviously, she'd heard their conversation.

The ice cream dripped on Tessa's foot, and she spun around to return to Loretta at the other end of the pool.

Maybe not the best start to Caro's new plan?

Carolina watched Tessa and Loretta chat, heads joined together, their gaze flitting toward the other side of the pool every few seconds.

11

Gossipfest

After a morning riding, and then an afternoon swimming, Carolina was wiped out. Her mom, who'd volunteered at the library every Friday, picked her up at the rec center. They grabbed pizza from Tony's, the one pizza place in town, and headed home.

They rode in silence, listening to her mom's instrumental Celtic music, pastures and hills rolling past them. Carolina's skin, red from the sun and chlorine, itched. So did her mind, worried about the future of Unbridled Dreams and the upcoming school year.

"What are you thinking about?" her mom asked, turning the music down.

Carolina worried that Tessa had told Loretta that she and

Brielle were talking about her. It was only a matter of time before this bit of gossip reached her archnemesis's ears and then her new idea about making things right with Loretta before school started would end in nothing. But she didn't want to tell her mom this. Instead, she talked about middle school, and how afraid she was that she wouldn't get to spend so much time with her friends if they had different classes.

"Then you'll have to find creative ways to spend time together," her mom said with a soothing smile.

When they arrived at the ranch, the strawberry full moon was just coming out from behind the mountains. Heather's truck and trailer were parked in front of the big barn, which meant Chelsie was back from her competition.

"Help me with the pizza and I'll take the books?" her mom asked, grabbing two full tote bags from the back seat.

"You have a good haul," Carolina said, trying to balance the boxes of pizza in her hands. The garlicky scent of Tony's secret sauce made her mouth water.

"I had to be ready for story times tomorrow," her mom said. "We have two sessions now."

"Two?"

"Yes! One for babies and one for older kids. I'm glad the read-to-a-horse program is growing even though we don't know if we'll get to sponsor more riding students in the fall. At least it's something we get to keep no matter what."

Carolina wished they could keep all the parts of Unbridled Dreams, but she didn't know how. Like every time she wanted time to think, she yearned to go down to the little barn. But her skin felt tight and tender from the day outside, and she was hungry.

Snuggling in Abuelita Ceci's arms sounded like a perfect alternative.

She was relishing this plan until she opened the door and saw everyone gathered around the kitchen table.

Everyone but her.

"Hi, my loves!" her dad said. He was letting his mustache grow again, and his salt-and-pepper hair was a little longer than usual. He stood, propping his leg on a chair, holding his guitar. "Now that my two favorite girls are here, we can start."

The room filled with smiles and hellos.

Chelsie, Vida, Jaime, and little Bracken sat around Abuela Ceci. A scattering of crafts littered the table. Boo was sitting at

Abuela Ceci's feet. He didn't even flick an ear when he heard Carolina's voice.

Carolina tried, she really did, to push down her jealousy. It's not like she hadn't had fun at the rec center.

But she felt a little left out.

"I was hoping to see you at the pool, Vida. What happened?" she said, trying to sound only curious and not hurt.

A cloud crossed Vida's eyes although she was smiling. "Today wasn't my day. I didn't feel like swimming, so I asked Luke to give me a ride here instead."

Luke was Jaime's older brother. They were Vida's cousins.

"And you, Bracken?" asked Carolina. "I thought you had turned into a goldfish for all the time you spend swimming."

His hair was the color of cornsilk, and his cheeks were rosy and covered with new freckles.

He smiled angelically. "My mom had to bring something for Poseidon, so I asked her if I could ride along. Jaime said his brother can give me a ride home." He glanced at Jaime. "Right, man?"

Jaime's eyes twinkled, but he didn't laugh. "Right."

"What did your mom have to bring?" Carolina asked.

Bracken shrugged. "She didn't say."

Carolina glanced at Chelsie. Maybe this had something to do with Loretta not going to the horse show in Boise as she'd planned? But if Chelsie had something to say, she wasn't going to do so in front of everyone.

"The pizza and garlic knots are going to get cold!" Abuela Ceci said, passing out plates for everyone to dig in.

"And the ice cream for dessert is going to melt!" Bracken exclaimed, scrunching up his nose.

It was so strange how much like Loretta he looked. They were siblings, of course, but he adored Carolina, and Loretta . . . well, Loretta didn't. But if the two had anything in common at all, maybe Carolina could find a way to relate to Loretta again.

Abuela Ceci handed her a plate with food, and Carolina moved to the problem at hand, namely, quieting down her growling stomach. She looked around for a place to sit, but the kitchen table was covered with multicolored beads and threads.

"What are you making?" Carolina asked, trying to sound happy.

"Friendship bracelets!" Vida said, beaming. "I made you one! Come sit next to me so I can tie it."

"Really?" A knot of sudden emotion grew in Carolina's throat.

She sat between Chelsie and Vida and admired the braided bracelet with beads that spelled Carolina's name. Caro had been feeling jealous, even though she had spent a fun day with new people. By the sound of it, Vida hadn't had a good time at cheer, and yet, here she was, carefully tying a bracelet around her wrist.

"Thank you," she said. "It's so kind of you to make one for me. You know I'm useless at these things."

Abuela Ceci smiled at her. "With a little patience you could learn."

"I wanted to make one for you, but Vida had started one first," Chelsie said. "So, I made matching ones for all of us that say *Unbridled Dreams*." She handed Carolina another bracelet, this one in pink and purple.

"Thank you, Chels."

There were a bunch of finished bracelets in the center of the table. Chelsie was so good at these things!

"Who are all those for?" Caro asked.

"We made one for every student, including Loretta," Bracken chimed in. "She hasn't been feeling too cheery lately." He clicked his tongue but didn't elaborate.

Carolina wanted to ask what he meant, but Jaime jumped in first.

"We made enough for even the volunteers and story-time people," Jaime said.

"Sorry I was gone and didn't help," Carolina said, grabbing a string and a handful of beads. She was determined to collaborate somehow.

"You were with Brielle!" Chelsie said. "You don't have to be at Paradise twenty-four seven to make sure things go according to plan. Remember we're a team."

Carolina sighed. "I know . . ."

"Do you get upset when Velvet and I are gone for competitions then?" Chelsie asked, narrowing her eyes.

"Of course not!" Caro said, playfully slapping the table and making the beads jump and roll to the floor. "Like the five Bs have taught me, I've learned to be a team player."

"It's settled then," Jaime said, tying up one more bracelet. "No more drama."

Caro's parents and Abuela Ceci exchanged a look like they were trying not to laugh.

"Weren't you about to sing, Papi?" Carolina said, trying to turn the spotlight away from her. "I don't want to wreck the plans for the night—"

"Stop it!" everyone exclaimed at once, and she laughed.

The adults moved to the kitchen island and the kids to the sofas, so they didn't have to move their crafts.

While they ate, Carolina brought them up to date on Brielle's progress. And then, trying not to sound like it was at the top of her mind, she asked about their schedules for the next year.

"The only thing I know is that we're in Spanish together. I asked my grandpa to check and make sure," Vida said. Her grandfather was the elementary school principal, which could be a pain, but it sure had its perks.

"I think we have the same English and Spanish classes, Caro," Chelsie said, pressing her hand.

"But don't worry about it," Jaime said. "The school's so big, you'll meet tons of new people, and you can also avoid those you don't like that much." He made a gesture toward Bracken.

"Bracken?" Carolina asked, but then she realized Jaime meant Loretta.

Bracken, who was only seven but sharp as a pin, caught his meaning too. He cleared his throat and said, "Don't be worried about my sister, Caro. Loretta might not even attend McAllister next year."

The silence that fell was thick and cold like a wet woolen blanket. They all eyed each other. The only one who didn't seem shocked was Chelsie, who seemed to be studying the pizza box.

"What do you mean?" Carolina asked, surprised at how dismayed she felt. Here she'd been thinking about making amends with Loretta, and now they weren't going to be in the same school?

"She has the chance to go to a boarding school with a good equestrian program. One in Montana," Bracken said. "That's why she didn't go to that show today. My parents are still figuring things out."

Carolina bit her lip, but the words were burning a hole through her tongue. "Loretta was at the pool, and she didn't seem very happy."

Chelsie stopped chewing and again looked at Caro through narrowed eyes. "Are you sure? She told me she was staying home because she had a headache."

Everyone's gaze turned to Bracken.

"Hold on a sec. I'm her brother, not a spy, okay?"

"You're right," Vida said, ruffling his dandelion fluff hair. "We wouldn't want you to reveal Loretta's secrets or anything."

Carolina turned to Chelsie, but she didn't know how to interpret the troubled look on her friend's face.

"What's wrong, Chels?"

Chelsie shrugged. "It's nothing . . ."

"Maybe because they had an argument," Bracken said.

"Bracken!" Chelsie said, pressing a finger to her lips for him to be quiet.

"She's right, Bracken. It's none of our business what your sister and Chelsie argued about," Carolina said, fighting to be the bigger person but hoping that Chelsie would still tell her.

"Ready for some music?" Caro's dad asked, the guitar back in his hands.

Everyone jumped to their feet and scurried to set the plates in the sink. They all loved it when he sang, but more than anything, it was a good excuse to break up the gossipfest.

12

New Neighbor

Kimber and Tyler were helping Heidi, the new horse, down from the trailer. The whole ranch had gathered to welcome them, but Carolina, in a rare bout of generosity, had decided to keep Shadow company.

In spite of her grand gesture, the Arabian was moping. Carolina didn't know how to lift his mood when she was struggling with hers. The news about Loretta moving to a boarding school, a fun one with an equestrian program, had upset her. She wasn't jealous, exactly. The idea of making up with Loretta had excited her, and now she wondered what the point of trying would be.

As she walked Shadow slowly around the arena the way Dr. Rooney had instructed, Carolina also wondered if all her efforts to help him were in vain too. The weekly injections hadn't made the effect they had expected, and the vet had reminded them that surgery might be the only way to help Shadow be pain free.

A few months ago, when Napoleon's health had been a little delicate, the whole ranch had tried to make sure to give him extra love in the shape of food and treats. But with Shadow, the situation was a little more complicated. They could make his problems worse by messing with his diet, so treats were out of the question. Although green grass was best for his situation, he always managed to get ahold of things he shouldn't eat when he went out in the large pastures.

For now Shadow had to stay in his stall or the small paddock beside it, which only made him sadder.

"I know you don't understand why this is happening to you," Carolina said, petting him as they finished his short daily walk. "But it's for your own good, sweetheart."

Even though she tried to convey all the love in her heart like Abuela Ceci had always taught her, Shadow didn't seem understand her intentions. He tossed his mane like the offended heroine in a soap opera.

On any other occasion, Carolina would laugh at his attitude. But now she was just sad.

"She's settled!" Chelsie exclaimed, running in Caro's direction.

Carolina turned to smile at her friend, but Chelsie still sensed her worry about Shadow.

"My mom said we can both help groom Heidi tonight. She needs a lot of TLC," Chelsie said, trying to cheer her up. "Come see!"

Carolina petted Shadow's neck. "Ready to meet your new neighbor?"

She followed Chelsie back to Shadow's stall and let the Arabian through his door. Heidi stood in the big box stall next door.

Like always, Carolina fell in love at first sight.

"She's a beauty," she said, smiling.

Heidi was a chestnut American quarter horse, the most common breed and color in the west. She was beautiful with her barely-rounder-than-usual tummy.

"You can tell she's had a challenging last few months," Chelsie said. "But Kimber said she's friendly and patient. She didn't pitch a fit even though the drive from Salt Lake was kind of long."

"Look at Twinkletoes and Leilani," Carolina said, pointing toward the pasture.

Chelsie chuckled. "Those two always notice the newcomers."

"I'm sure they'll all get along. Look how curious they look," Carolina said.

"Yes, but Kimber said that until the baby is born, it's safer to keep Heidi away from the main herd. We'll introduce her and the foal slowly to the other horses to make sure they all get along."

Later, in the afternoon, when Carolina went out to feed Luna, she was pleasantly surprised to see that Heidi and Shadow had seemed to form a friendship across their shared fence. They communicated in snorts, touches, and nickers. Maybe they'd decided that befriending each other was better than being alone.

After all, horses, like people, are social animals, and they thrive in groups.

Carolina hoped that Shadow would still be at Paradise when it was safe for the baby to meet the rest of the horses.

· U ·

A couple of weeks later when Brielle arrived for her lesson, she found Caro and Chelsie sitting on bales of hay in the little barn. They were trying to think of how to save money for Shadow's surgery, which Heather had decided had become a necessity. His owners didn't want to pay for it, so Heather had hesitantly committed to buying him and taking on the cost. Even though they couldn't cover it yet.

Tyler, Kimber, and Caro's and Chelsie's parents had pooled some money together. Even Carolina's uncle Achilles had sent a check from New Mexico. But it still wasn't near enough to pay for everything Shadow needed.

"Even if I sell everything I own, it'll hardly make a difference," Carolina said, scribbling out the long list she'd started in her notebook of things she could live without.

"What are you saving money for?" Brielle asked.

Carolina, whose head was pounding with the injustice of having to do math during summer vacation, looked at Chelsie, begging for her to take over.

Chelsie explained the situation. Always so efficient by going straight to the point.

Brielle scratched her head and said, "Earning the whole amount at once is impossible. But what if we break it up into little goals, like the Five Bs teach?" She narrowed her eyes, deep in thought.

"Brilliant!" Carolina replied.

"Girls! Help Brielle with Marigold, please!" Kimber called from outside.

Although Kimber had said Brielle would work on Napoleon again, they didn't question the change of plans. They all got to work right away in gathering the tack and going out to get Marigold ready for her lesson.

"We have all day to plan, right?" Brielle said, enthusiastically as she combed leaves out of Marigold's dark mane.

It was true.

They were all heading to the rec center in the afternoon. This time even Chelsie was ready to join them, even if she only stayed in the shallow end.

In the outdoor ring, Brielle was still determined to get Marigold to gallop, but the mustang was even more stubborn than Shadow and kept to a trot, which was what Kimber wanted anyway. At least Brielle didn't get distracted as she had in the first few lessons, and she remembered to be patient with herself.

"Good job staying present, Brielle!" Kimber said.

Brielle rolled her eyes. "But I can't get the rhythm to post," she said, disappointed.

"Little by little, you're going to get it. You'll see," the trainer assured her.

When Brielle dismounted, Carolina tried to be her useful cheerful self, but she couldn't help but think of Shadow all alone in his stall.

A part of her told her not to think of the worst-case scenario. But . . . it was so hard not to think that if they couldn't pay for his surgery, and his owners decided not to keep him . . . he would be sent to the auction.

And every horse girl knew what an auction could mean: a chance at a good family or, heaven forbid, kill-pen buyers.

Carolina was glad that Heidi and her foal had ended up in a safe place. But at the same time, she had to admit she wished that they had bought Shadow before they'd adopted the rescue horse!

On the way to town, Carolina noticed the *For Sale* signs in the front of houses or next to mailboxes had grown like mushrooms under fallen logs.

"Look! They're building a subdivision at Mitchell's Peaches!" Chelsie exclaimed, pointing.

Mitchell's Peaches was a property as old as Paradise Ranch. They'd driven too fast to see exactly what the developers had planned for the piece of land, but Carolina caught a glimpse of the small plots and the stock picture of a smiling family in front of a house.

Her heart tugged in so many conflicting directions. Her feelings intensified when she saw Loretta sitting at her usual spot by the pool. Carolina hadn't yet taken the plunge to try making up with Loretta. She still wasn't sure how. And anyway, Loretta hadn't been around at the ranch to exercise Poseidon lately. Bracken had taken over cleaning his stall and feeding the horse, but most of the time, Tyler did it. What would happen if she went to that boarding school? Would her family find a new place for Poseidon too or would Loretta get to take him along?

For all the conflicts she'd had with Loretta, she had to admit that with Loretta gone, Paradise wouldn't be the same.

Vida, Chelsie, and Brielle gathered around Carolina. With so many friends—finally—maybe she didn't need Loretta.

"We need to do all we can to help Shadow," Brielle said, taking her Unbridled Dreams journal and a pen from her backpack.

"How though?" Chelsie asked.

The little kids splashed and played in the pool, but the group of girls intently wracked their brains for something, anything they could do.

"What if we do a bake sale at the farmers market?"

"A bake sale!" exclaimed Vida. "And we can add crafts!"

That little spark of an idea gave way to a wildfire of inspiration.

"Face paint!"

"Babysitting!"

"Pony rides!"

Carolina had strong opinions about pony rides at carnivals, but then her mind lit up. "What about photos with a mini donkey!"

They all cheered. Loretta's eyes flew in their direction, but Carolina ignored her.

"Operation Save Shadow," Vida said, and Brielle wrote the words in big bubble letters at the top of the page.

"We have a goal. We have action plans. Now we need a time line," Chelsie said.

They all turned to Carolina.

"The big auction is the day before the summer parade on August fifteenth. We should've started saving as soon as we found out he might need surgery. We shouldn't have wasted so much time . . ."

"Like my mom always says, the best day to start is always today," Brielle said.

"I have a few competitions at the end of July, but for now I'm free," Chelsie said.

"Good thing cheer training is off until the first week of school. Count me in," said Vida.

"Same!" added Brielle.

"Awesome! We can start on Friday for the farmers market. Everyone text me or . . ." Chelsie looked at Caro, the only one who didn't have a cell phone. "Or call me and tell me what you're contributing for the sale. What we earn, we use to buy supplies for the crafts. And the rest we put into the Shadow fund. You'll see, we'll get the money."

Their enthusiasm was contagious. Carolina had some hope for the first time since she'd heard the news. But then Chelsie looked toward the other side of the pool and saw Loretta. Her smile vanished.

"Chelsie? Is everything okay?" Carolina asked, trying to find the right words. "I've been trying not to pry, but are you and Loretta in a fight since she's going to that school next year?"

Chelsie sighed. "We didn't fight, exactly. But she's been . . . weird about the whole thing and she won't talk to me."

"Why? Is she pretending she's a better rider than you or something?"

Chelsie rolled her eyes. "She's *always* thought she's a better rider than everyone else. I don't even want to imagine the size of her head when she comes back from that fancy school to visit. That's not what it is this time. I don't know what her deal is. She's pushing everyone away. Even Tessa."

Carolina had noticed that too. Lately at the pool, Loretta had been by herself instead of with the usual posse of fangirls. Maybe they should tell her about the plan to save Shadow. But if Loretta was going to leave anyway, what was the point in getting close to her now?

13

Operation Save Shadow Begins

A couple of nights later at the little barn, Carolina and Chelsie were planning what to make for the bake sale. They had pulled out tack to clean while they chatted tonight.

"Nothing chocolaty or it will melt," Chelsie said, polishing Velvet's saddle for a competition that would take place in a few days.

Chocolate chip with instant coffee mixed in was the only kind of cookies that Caro knew how to make. Abuela Ceci had sent her the recipe a few months ago, and after some—okay, several—failed attempts, Carolina's concoctions were starting to resemble cookies. At least they tasted delicious.

If chocolate was out of the question, then what could she make?

"Oatmeal raisin cookies?" Caro suggested. "I love the ones at school."

"I think you're the only kid in the whole wide world who likes that kind," Chelsie teased her.

They laughed so loud Bella snorted as if reminding them that some people (namely horses) were trying to sleep. Which made them laugh even more.

"We can try. You know how people miss things from school as soon as summer break starts. Even the things they complain about all year," Caro said as she went back to oiling Leilani's harness.

"It's true," Chelsie said. "We waited for summer all year, and now it's here, we're just ready for fall and winter."

"It's the circle of life, baby," Caro said. "And you've almost completed your first year around it at Paradise, horse girl!"

Chelsie smiled, contented. "Does that mean I'm a proper country girl now?"

Carolina was going to say that she was still far from that, considering the pearl earrings, the pink polished nails, and the fringed boots Chelsie was rocking. But even then . . . yes, Chelsie had become a country girl.

"You get up early for chores and stay up late for them. You know where food comes from. You're even starting to like country music . . ." Carolina paused for a dramatic effect, which landed right on target.

"Am not!" Chelsie said, rolling her eyes. But her cheeks flushed.

She had been listening to country when Carolina had come into the barn.

"I didn't want to waste time looking for another CD. Besides, I was being nice, since you always listen to Velvet Lilly and never complain."

Carolina was glad her friend had noticed that she had really been trying for almost a year not to act like the ranch belonged to her. And she could see that Chelsie, whose mom actually owned everything, was doing just the same. They both lived here, and they both took care of things, animals, and people with the same love and care. There were moments when Carolina wished she had a saddle with her name engraved on it, like Chelsie did, but that was the least of her worries.

Trying to come up with something she could contribute to the bake sale, Carolina sighed and placed the rag on the floor so it wouldn't leave a grease stain on her favorite work pants. She wasn't the fancy kind of horse girl Chelsie was, but she took care of her appearance in her own way.

And then she had an idea.

· U ·

Paradise had a quaint little downtown, with about two blocks of shops in each direction spanning from the giant park in its center.

Since it was on the route to Yellowstone to the north and the Utah national parks in the south, it was a popular stop for trucks, vans, and campers. They got a lot of traffic in the summer. Especially for their famous farmers market.

With the scent of barbecue from one of the food trucks and the sound of people gathering to exchange news and good times, the farmers market was its own destination. A folksy string band played music under the shade of the gazebo on Main Street, and a few young kids danced together while their parents talked.

It was a perfect summer Saturday morning even if the sky was a little hazy from forest fires in Montana.

Hopeful, Carolina and Chelsie unloaded their wares from Heather's SUV, and they headed to the booth Caro's mom had reserved for them.

Brielle and Vida were already waiting. They had set up a table and a canopy. On the table there was an assortment of brownies, cookies, and cupcakes. Carolina was grateful she'd had the idea of selling chocolate chip cookie mix! It was the perfect solution for the heat.

Knowing that at the mansion house at Paradise, Chelsie and her mom were making complicated cake pops, Carolina had been determined to stretch her abilities to collaborate with something pretty.

It was all for Shadow, after all, so she had to try her best.

When Mrs. Parry had moved out of the mansion house, she'd left cases and cases of tiny, cute jars that she had used to can apple sauce from the apples that had grown in the orchard that had given Paradise its first name, the original one: Orchard Farms. With time, it had become more of a horse operation, and then when the Parrys moved away, they'd left behind a lot of things they would have no more use for. Like canning jars.

Carolina had washed them with hot soapy water. Once they were dry, she filled them carefully with the mix she'd created in large batches with her abuela. Then she added directions on how to prepare the cookies on cute postcards that her mom printed out for her. The Unbridled Dreams logo was at the top of the page, and on the back, she even had room to add the Five Bs.

"Great idea!" Abuela Ceci had said. "These are principles that people, especially children, can apply to improve their lives. It's a little gift. You never know the reach that words can have, mi amor. Maybe someone who can never take classes will come across the Bs, apply them, and that can send their lives on a whole different course."

Carolina considered the power of what she and Chelsie had started.

Who would have said a year ago that a mistake like trying to train a skittish thoroughbred on their own would lead to impacting people's lives? Even people she might never know.

The thought kept her optimistic as she placed her jars on the table and tried not to compare them to the things her friends had brought. The cake pops Chelsie had made were the cutest and most eye-catching item, with their pink icing and glimmering sprinkles. Still, Carolina was proud of how careful she'd been to cut rounds of leftover fabrics and place them on top of the jar lids; she'd found pretty ribbons to secure the lids and hang the recipe cards from.

Vida had brought cupcakes, and Brielle had made three kinds of cookies. Even Bracken had shown up with a tray of brownies and another one of Rice Krispie squares. For a second, Carolina thought Loretta might be joining them, but the blond girl walked away from the booth as soon as Bracken seemed settled. But then no one had invited Loretta into the plan to save Shadow.

Caro had no time to waste on thinking about Loretta though. Soon, customers started arriving.

The cupcakes, cake pops, and cookies flew off the table.

Abuela Ceci had the idea to bring a jar of her delicious aguas frescas for them to gift along with every baked product. Everyone was so grateful, they left generous tips in their jar.

But Carolina's cookie-mix jars stayed untouched on the table. Maybe her grand idea hadn't been so grand after all.

Her heart could only take so much rejection. She didn't

want to cry in front of everyone, so she grabbed one of the posters announcing their products and prices and went to the corner of the park.

Across the street, Loretta was standing by herself, eating an ice-cream cone.

Carolina hesitated but then waved.

Loretta squinted and leaned forward as if she was trying to figure out if Carolina was waving hello or waving her over.

Carolina gulped when she saw Loretta walking in her direction.

"Hey," Loretta said, smirking. Or maybe by now this was the permanent expression on her face.

"Hey," Carolina replied. For some strange reason, her heart was pounding as she tried to think of what to say next. She considered asking if Loretta wanted to join the rest of the group in their booth, or if she wanted to hold one end of the poster and keep Carolina company.

"What flavor did you get?" she finally asked.

Loretta licked her ice cream like she hadn't even noticed what flavor she'd ordered and then said, "Honeysuckle."

That was one of Carolina's favorites. The shop had other

unique flavors like boysenberry, corn, and lavender. If she wasn't trying to save every last penny for Shadow, then she might be tempted to go grab one herself.

The music from the musicians stopped for a minute, accentuating the awkward silence between the girls.

"You have sunscreen on your nose," Loretta said, pointing with her ice cream-free hand. But she didn't offer to help Carolina wipe it off or anything. Instead, she added, "I didn't know people like you need sunscreen too."

Carolina was too stunned to reply. Loretta could only have meant because Caro's skin was darker than hers. What was it about Loretta that made the words turn to ashes on her lips?

"Of course we do," Carolina finally spluttered. "Everyone has to protect themselves from the sun."

Loretta seemed unaware that she'd said anything offensive. She shrugged. "Like I said, I didn't know."

Without saying another word, Loretta crossed the street back to the ice-cream shop and sat all alone at one of the round tables. She took out her phone and started scrolling.

Carolina tried to pretend Loretta wasn't there, but she felt the other girl's gaze on her.

Self-conscious and feeling off-kilter from Loretta's comment, she almost turned back to the booth and gave up her plan. When Loretta saw her, she would think Carolina looked ridiculous. What if she made a video and put it online? But Shadow was worth everything, even the risk of humiliation. Finally, Carolina took her old Discman out of her backpack, which held one of her favorite mix CDs that included reggaeton, rock en español, country, and her favorite Velvet Lilly songs.

She placed the earbuds in her ears, turned the volume all the way up to quiet her doubts and insecurities, and started dancing, twirling the *Sale* sign.

14

Everything Adds Up

Later that evening, Carolina could almost pretend she hadn't done the unthinkable and danced in front of the whole town. Worse, in front of Loretta. Even though Loretta and her friends had called her "Aguasmuertas" just months ago for her infamous two left feet, she'd still done it.

And it had been worth it.

"Wow!" exclaimed Abuela Ceci when Carolina and Chelsie showed her the money they had earned. "That's impressive! Congratulations!"

"It's all because of Caro's bravery," Chelsie said. "From not wanting to dance in the end-of-the-year festival to standing on the corner waving our sign around! Way to go, Caro!"

Carolina blushed and laughed as she remembered how she

had stood on the corner all morning, dancing and making fancy throws and maneuvers with the sign as she got more comfortable. Her arms were achy from her improvised chore-ography. Vida was right! Dancing was tiring!

A few minutes into her dance routine when she'd peeked across the street to see if Loretta was still there, she couldn't find her. Which was just as well.

Benji Clark, one of the coolest boys at school, had laughed when he saw Carolina, but still headed to the treat table. A few minutes later, he walked back past Caro holding a handful of cake pops and two jars of cookie mix!

By noon, they'd sold out of almost everything. There was just one jar left, and Carolina had brought it back home to make cookies for tonight's campfire.

"Now we have money to buy supplies for crafts," Caro said. "If we add the goodies to the crafts, then we'll get the money sooner than we expected."

A few days later, Brielle donated some money she'd earned babysitting to the Shadow Rescue Fund.

"Is that okay?" Chelsie asked Caro. "Is it fair for her?"

"We need to ask our moms, but I think it's okay," Carolina said.

Heather spoke with Brielle's mom who said she was happy her daughter was volunteering for a great cause.

The next morning while they mucked the stalls, Chelsie said, "Maybe we can babysit too."

"I've never taken care of babies," Carolina replied. She liked babies and little kids, but she had no experience caring for them, having grown up as an only daughter.

"There's a babysitting class at the rec center. They give you a certificate."

"I didn't know you needed a certificate!" Carolina exclaimed, surprised. But then she thought that if to take care of animals, volunteers needed to be trained, then for human kids, it made sense that babysitters had to train too.

"Do you think there's anything else we could do?" she asked.

The answer came the following week when the phone rang just as Carolina was heading to check on Shadow.

"Hello, Aguasvivas residence," Carolina said in what she hoped was a professional voice. She had a brief flashback to

Tessa making fun of her once, saying the cottage wasn't a residence.

On the other end of the phone, an older man said, "Oh, hello. My name is Mr. Wong, and I was wondering if your group of friends would like to help me clean a vacant lot I have. One of your girls, Brielle was her name, said you were collecting money for a horse. I could pay for help mowing the lawn and getting rid of weeds."

Carolina's heart about jumped from her chest. "Yes! Tell me the address and we'll be there."

She grabbed a pen and paper from next to the phone and took notes.

"I'll get a group organized and we'll call you back to coordinate the time," she said, a battle raging in her mind. She wanted to ask how much he could pay them but didn't dare.

"That sounds good," Mr. Wong said, and then, before he hung up, he added, "I had a horse when I was a young boy, and we couldn't afford to send him to the vet for a procedure. I remember what that feels like, and I don't have money to spare, but instead of paying a landscaper, I thought it would be a fair trade." He told her the amount he could afford to pay. It wasn't nearly as much as they needed for Shadow, but it would make another dent. Besides, she was moved by the man's gesture.

"Thank you for your generosity, Mr. Wong."

Abuela Ceci arrived just as Carolina was hanging up. She must have sensed the feelings bubbling inside Carolina because she asked, "Who was that on the phone? Vida?"

Carolina smiled at her and said, "It was a customer, Abuela!"

She quickly updated her on the conversation. But then, when Abuela Ceci asked how much Mr. Wong was going to pay them, her enthusiasm fizzled out.

"What's wrong, mi amor?" Abuela asked, lifting Carolina's chin with her index finger. There was nowhere to hide her feelings now. Abuela Ceci could read her like an open book.

"Mr. Wong is very generous, but we're still short of the money Shadow needs."

"Everything adds up," Abuela Ceci said. "You never know the other unexpected rewards that can come your way."

"Like what?"

"Like learning to work hard for a goal, even if the outcome isn't guaranteed. There's power in stretching yourself beyond your limits. There's also power when you do your best, still come out short, but learn to be at peace with that. I'm happy that you're learning to work well with others. When we work together, we achieve more than we could ever dream on our own. Those are all very valuable lessons to learn when you're still so young, my love."

"I just want everything to be okay," Carolina said, her voice tiny and worried.

"Everything will be okay in the end, and if things aren't okay, then it isn't the end," Abuela said, and kissed Carolina's forehead.

Abuela Ceci's words soothed Carolina's fears, but at the same time, a little voice in the back of her mind whispered one more thing she could be doing.

By not including Loretta and her friends in saving Shadow, they were all missing out. Especially Shadow.

Carolina didn't know if they could make up, or if it would be worth it with Loretta leaving soon. Would reaching out a hand of friendship even work?

She would only have to try or she'd never know.

· U ·

Carolina whistled at the tangle of weeds and vines in front of her. She hadn't touched a shovel yet, but a bead of sweat ran down her forehead under her Unbridled Dreams cap. It was already a hot day, and Mr. Wong hadn't been kidding. The lot in question looked like several acres of land overridden by weeds.

This was a fire hazard!

After her chat with Abuela Ceci, Carolina had almost called Loretta to see if she wanted to join the cleanup but changed her mind at the last minute. She regretted it now. They could've used all the help they could get. This was a big job, and the day was so hot.

Chelsie was gone at another show, but Carolina had eventually roped Jaime into helping. He knew how to use a lawn mower, and the boys from his football team had muscle power. His brother Luke had just delivered her and Jaime to the lot, where Vida and Brielle were already waiting.

"You owe me after this, Caro," Jaime said beside her, but he didn't sound upset.

"It's for a good cause," she reminded him. And herself.

Mr. Wong was there with tools for them to use. "I've been coming by to take care of it every few weeks, but my back isn't what it used to be," he said as he showed Jaime the lawn mower. "I can't do it on my own anymore."

"We're happy to help! Thanks for calling us," Carolina said, hoping she could deliver on her promise of doing a good job.

The kids got right to work. A couple of hours later, Bracken, who lived a block away, brought a giant jug of water on his wagon, and everyone sat under the shade of a large tree for a break. They'd made a lot of progress, but they were far from finished.

Once she'd gulped down a couple cups of water, Carolina went back to weeding an overgrown pumpkin patch. She was determined to finish before the evening.

She wore gloves, extra wary of the thorns. Still, her skin was soon itchy with sweat and dust. Without thinking, she took off one of her gloves to scratch a spot on her neck that was driving her bananas. With the tips of her fingers, she noticed small bumps on her skin. She looked at her arm where she felt the same kind of itchiness, and to her horror, she saw a trail of angry-looking raised bumps.

Hives.

Her face felt like it was on fire, and when she opened her mouth to call for help, her lip felt swollen. It was just like that time she'd borrowed Chelsie's lip gloss to find out it was Heather's lip plumper instead. Only ten times worse. Cold sweat ran down her spine when she saw the angry red patches covering her arms.

"Guys!" she called, trying not to alarm anyone. But she felt like when she was five and had gathered a bunch of poison ivy because the red hue looked pretty. She wasn't pretty for weeks after that. But from then on, she was always so careful not to touch any poisonous leaves, repeating the preschool rhyme "Leaves of three, let it be." She was sure she hadn't seen any poison ivy today!

The thorn from that wild apple tree that was still deep in her thumb started to pulse. She'd become used to living with that irritation, but it was still there. And now her whole body throbbed with pain.

"Ah!" she said, yanking off the other glove to scratch herself.

Brielle saw her first.

"Caro!" she exclaimed. "We need to call for help! You have hives on your face!"

Carolina's mom was back at the ranch, and Luke had gone to get sandwiches for everyone. Mr. Wong had also gone home for a little bit. Since Jaime was done using the lawn mower, no one was supervising them. They were just pulling weeds.

Carolina panicked.

Just in that moment, Bracken arrived, sweat pouring down his little face as he pulled the water wagon for the second time. When he saw her, he said, "You need help right now! You're having an allergic reaction!"

15

This Town Ain't Big Enough
for the Two of Us

"I'm okay, Bracken," Carolina said, but she was alarmed at the urgency in his voice.

Vida's eyes widened when she saw Carolina's face.

"It's that bad, huh?" Carolina asked, trying not to cry.

Vida nodded as she texted quickly.

Meanwhile, Bracken dropped the handle of his wagon and said, "Let's go to my house! My mom will know what to do!"

Carolina took a couple breaths. If Loretta was home, then Carolina didn't want her to see her like this.

But this was no time to be picky.

"Come on! If it's a real allergy, it can be dangerous!" Brielle said.

She didn't know if it was the allergic reaction or dehydration making saliva pool in her mouth, but suddenly, she felt queasy.

She would not throw up in front of the middle school football team. It was enough that they'd seen her looking hideous.

She nodded. "Okay. Let's go."

Jaime lifted the heavy water jug from the wagon, Brielle and Vida carefully placed Caro in it, and enlisting the football team, all together, they hauled her toward the Sullivans' house as fast as they could go.

· U ·

Modern medicines are a miracle, and Carolina was grateful she'd put her pride aside and followed Bracken's suggestion to head to his house.

"Take this, sweetheart," Mrs. Sullivan said, giving Carolina another tablet of antihistamine. It was the same kind that Vida took for her hay fever. "Your mom is on her way, but she said it's okay for you to take another dose of this."

Obediently, Carolina took the tablet, swallowed it, and chased it with a couple gulps of water. She didn't know if the medicine worked so fast, but she thought the itching was less severe.

"I don't know what I touched," Carolina said. Her throat felt raspy. "I was careful."

"Weren't you in the pumpkin patch?" Bracken asked, scratching his head.

"Yes," said Carolina, "but I had gloves."

"If you brush the stems of certain plants, you can still get a reaction. I remember your dad has a skin sensitivity to potato peels, right?" Mrs. Sullivan said, giving Carolina a glass of orange juice.

Carolina nodded.

"Then I'm sure that's it," she said. "Now, Bracken, go out and give an update to all the kids waiting outside. You, Caro, sit here. I'll be right back."

Bracken and his mom left, and Carolina sat quietly in the Sullivans' fancy kitchen.

Fancy for Caro, at least. The appliances weren't brand-new,

shiny chrome like at Chelsie's, but they were much newer than the ones at the cottage. Not that Chelsie's mom hadn't offered to remodel their house too, but Caro's parents had declined. They loved the cozy house as it was.

She drank more juice but almost spit it out when someone opened the kitchen half door—the slatted kind, like in a western saloon in the movies—and Loretta walked into the kitchen, strutting like the sheriff.

"What are you doing here?" she asked, startled when she saw Carolina.

Carolina was already frazzled, and honestly, a little scared. She was so mixed up because she shouldn't have excluded Loretta from the plan to save Shadow, but Loretta's rudeness kept stopping Carolina from reaching out.

Loretta seemed to regret her outburst once she assessed the situation.

"Are you okay?" she whispered, sounding worried. "Your face is all . . . puffy."

"I got an allergic reaction to pumpkin vines. Bracken and the other kids got scared when they saw the hives."

"What were you doing in the old pumpkin patch? And what do you mean Bracken and the other kids?" Loretta's face was red, like she too was having an allergic reaction: to being left out.

Carolina's words tumbled out. "We're saving money for Shadow's surgery, and Mr. Wong asked if we'd help him pull weeds and mow the grass in his vacant lot."

Loretta peeked out the window, and when she saw the kids gathered in the shade, she said, "I would've helped if you had asked me."

Carolina felt a pain in the center of her chest.

"Why did you come here?" Loretta asked.

Carolina had agreed to come to Bracken's—and Loretta's—house because even though the girls weren't friends anymore, she knew their mom would help. Like Loretta would've helped if Carolina had asked her to join forces for Shadow's sake.

But she didn't know how to say all that without crying, so she swallowed her words.

She got up to leave. "Don't worry. I'll leave as soon as my mom arrives. I'll go wait for her outside if you want."

"No," Loretta said, and grabbed the back of Carolina's shirt as she walked toward the door.

The sound of ripping fabric thundered in the kitchen above the lulling sound of the dishwasher and the clock ticking on the wall. Above Carolina's pounding heart.

In that moment, Mrs. Sullivan walked into the kitchen, followed by Bracken and a man who wore a suit and tie. In this heat!

She saw that Carolina's shirt was torn, and her gaze zeroed in on Loretta.

"I . . . It's not . . ." Loretta said, blushing furiously.

"Oh my," said the man when he saw Carolina's shirt was torn in the back. At least she had a swimsuit underneath since Brielle had wanted to go to the pool after.

Bracken gasped and his hands flew to his mouth in horror.

"Please go to your room," Loretta's mom ordered, leaving no room for disagreement or explanations. As Loretta disappeared through the doorway, her mom said to Bracken, "Please give Caro one of the shirts from the laundry. It doesn't matter which one. Sorry, Caro." She turned toward the man and said, "Please, follow me to the sitting room. Life with children, you know how it is."

The man nodded as if he knew too well and sat on the sofa in front of the TV.

A minute later, Bracken came back and handed Carolina a T-shirt that was still warm from the dryer. "Sorry, Caro. I'm sure Loretta didn't mean to. She's been grumpy, but she's not evil."

Carolina knew Loretta hadn't meant to rip her shirt. But why had she tried to stop her from going out?

Vida, who'd been waiting outside, came in through the back door and said, "Caro, your mom's here."

She saw the ripped back of Caro's shirt and furrowed her forehead.

Then, hearing voices, she looked up and saw the man; her eyes widened.

"I'll tell you later," Carolina whispered.

Carolina didn't want to explain to her mom why her shirt was ripped, so she walked into the bathroom and changed quickly before going outside.

Not now, but when she recovered from her allergic

reaction and her wounded ego, Carolina had to talk to Loretta and clear things up with her once and for all. Even if she wasn't going to attend the same school, this feud couldn't keep pestering their lives like the infected thorn in her hand.

16

Mystery Man

It took a while for the hives to heal, and combined with the effects of dry, smoky air, Carolina's skin was itchier than ever.

"Maybe take a break from the pool for a few days," her mom said.

Carolina didn't even have the heart to argue. She was frustrated that they'd been on a roll with fundraising for Shadow, and then this had happened.

Bored of watching TV when the day was so gorgeous, she went outside and sat in the shade of a tree next to the little barn.

"Life is unfair," she said.

Luna the cat, who was lounging on one of the branches

above her, only blinked in reply, but it looked like she agreed. If life were fair, she wouldn't have to listen to Caro's complaints.

Boo had preferred to stay in the coolness of the cottage. Abuela Ceci was in town buying groceries with Jaime, and Chelsie had gone to a competition. Again.

With all the stablehands busy, Carolina felt like in the olden times. Lonely, with only the animals for company.

Last year Carolina had been more than happy to spend time just with the horses. But now? Now she missed her friends.

Carolina couldn't help but feel that time was running away from her. Nothing she did seemed to make a dent in the money they needed for Shadow. And no matter what she did to support Brielle, and make sure she had a great experience at Unbridled Dreams, Carolina couldn't keep the sponsorship program running all by herself. That, too, required money she didn't have. She didn't even want to think about her rift with Loretta.

She looked at Shadow and Heidi having a conversation across their shared fence. Marigold and Bella and Leilani took turns grooming each other's backs in the bright sunlight. Two of the boarding horses rolled on the grass.

And then a car arrived. Carolina turned at the sound of the gravel and watched the silver sedan roll past her. Even before the man got out of the driver's seat, she recognized his suit. He'd been at the Sullivans!

Who was he, and what did he want?

He knocked on the door of the mansion house and waited and waited, but no one came out. No one was home, after all.

Relentless, the smiling man looked around and saw the house at the top of the hill. It was the first building that welcomed everyone into the property. He had to have seen it when he drove down the driveway, but it was obvious that it was a caretaker's building and not where the owners lived.

The man scratched his dark hair.

Carolina couldn't be sure because he wore dark sunglasses that, along with his mustache, hid most of his face, but she thought he looked like he was thinking about going up to the cottage. To her house. He went back to the car.

Carolina breathed with relief thinking that he was going to keep driving up to the state road. Instead, the car stopped at the top of the hill and the man came out to knock at the cottage door.

Boo's barks reached all the way to where Carolina was now standing, her body vibrating with anticipation and the dilemma booming in her mind.

Maybe her dad had gone back to work; she hadn't seen him, and her mom had headed to the office. Maybe they didn't hear the knock at the door and the man would drive away again.

Should Carolina just let him go and pretend no one had seen him stop by their ranch? Or should she go up and ask what he needed?

Her heart pounded so hard and painfully, she thought she was going to get sick if she stayed standing like a tree.

The door opened and her dad greeted the man pleasantly, like he always did. The man pointed toward the mansion house, and then gave her dad an envelope and drove away.

Carolina's dad remained standing at the door of the cottage, as if he too had grown roots. As if he too were unsure of what to do next. Probably feeling her eyes on him, he saw her by the willow tree and waved.

That's all Carolina needed to make up her mind and run home.

·U·

"Who was he? What did he want?" she asked as soon as her feet crossed the front threshold. A cloud of dust had enveloped her as she ran.

Her dad showed her an envelope. "It's for Heather," he said.

The swamp cooler blew nice, humid, cool air on her face, but Carolina felt like she was burning.

"What do you think it's about?"

Her dad looked at her with a glint of a warning in his face. "Caro . . ."

She sighed, embarrassed for being so nosy, and dropped on the couch dramatically. Boo didn't waste any time and ran to rest his head on her knee, demanding she pet him. She complied. "I saw him at the Sullivans' the day I got the allergic reaction."

Her dad sat next to her. "I hope you weren't eavesdropping."

She sat up and narrowed her eyes at him. "Of course I wasn't! You raised me better than that."

"Good" was all he said, but he continued looking at her as if he knew she wasn't done with the conversation.

But Carolina wanted to change the subject.

"We made a lot of money with our sales and the yard cleaning," she said. "A lot of people want to help Shadow."

A lot of people she hadn't even included . . . People like Loretta. But she didn't say that.

"That's fantastic," Papi said, and then he took a deep breath. He hesitated, and Caro knew that what he was about to say was going to hurt. But she'd rather hear it from him.

"What is it, Papi?" she placed a hand on his.

Papi smiled and ruffled her hair. "What do you want for your birthday?"

Carolina was taken by surprise with the change of subject. "My birthday?"

"It's still at the end of July like it is every year, right?" he asked, and laughed.

In that moment, Mom walked downstairs.

"Tell us, Caro," Mom said. "We can't figure out what to give you for your birthday."

Carolina thought. Not because she didn't know what to ask for, but because there were so many things she wanted. At the top of her list was for Shadow to get better and stay with them or at least find a good home.

But that wasn't something her parents could get her.

Carolina bit her lip.

"What, Caro?" Papi asked.

She looked up at him, and said, "It feels . . . wrong to spend money on anything when Shadow needs every cent we can save. We still need money for his surgery."

"Caro . . ." her mom said, hugging her with one arm. "It's still okay to buy food to eat, get clothes for school, enjoy your life. Remember, live in the present."

"I'm trying, Ma," she said. "It's hard to live in the present *and* plan for the future." She rubbed her forehead. "It makes my head hurt."

"Don't worry about too many things. It will all work out," Mom said. "Now, why don't you invite a few friends for a party?"

A party? She hadn't had one in a while. She knew exactly who to invite. She'd start with the hardest name on her list. Even if she said no, it was the right thing to do.

· ∪ ·

The phone rang three times, echoing against Carolina's ear and the walls of her room. She nervously twirled a pen with a mini horse on the end. When she was about to give up and hang up, Loretta's voice replied, "Hello?"

"Oh, hi, Loretta," Carolina said before she lost her nerve and the words fled from her mind and lips again. "It's Carolina."

"I know it's you," Loretta said in that infuriating tone of voice. But then, she added in a softer tone, "Bracken's at the pool. He'll be back soon though, if you want to call him back."

Carolina cleared her throat and said, "Actually, I wanted to talk to you. If that's okay." She closed her eyes and crossed her fingers.

Hoping the silence at the other end of the line meant that it was okay, Carolina said, "I wanted to say sorry for not including you in the plans to save Shadow." Her heart pounded in her ears, and she braced herself for a click that would indicate Loretta had hung up on her.

Instead, Loretta said, "I'm sorry I ripped your shirt. And for the rude comment I made about the sunscreen." She swallowed. "Sometimes I don't even know why I get in a nasty mood, and I take it out on everyone."

Carolina hadn't expected an apology from Loretta, but now that she had one, it felt like when her mom applied aloe vera on her sunburned skin: cooling and soothing. She hoped that her own apology had the same effect on Loretta too.

There were so many things she wanted to ask, like whether it was true that Loretta was leaving to boarding school, or why their friendship had died after that summer camp in Boise. But she had called specifically for something, so she said, "I also wanted to see if you want to come over for a party on my birthday. I can invite Tessa too, if you want."

There was another pause. It seemed both girls were being extra careful with the things they said and how they said it.

"Thanks, but I can't," Loretta said, and Carolina's spirits dropped. Oh well. She had tried. She'd tried to put their enmity behind. That had to count for something, right?

"The reason I can't is because I'll be out of town that day. But I'm glad you invited me. Happy birthday, Caro."

Carolina was sad that Loretta wouldn't make it after all, but the conversation had given her hope. Loretta had even remembered what day her birthday was.

"Thanks, Lori," she said, and hung up.

17

Stillwater Equestrian Academy

The next week, after they'd finished all the plans for Carolina's birthday party, she and Chelsie were watching Brielle and Vida in a combined class. It had been Chelsie's idea so they could help each other out.

Both girls could now tack the horses without help, switch directions, and communicate with unspoken commands. Today they were working on posting the trot. Vida in a Western saddle, and Brielle in English.

Unsurprisingly, Brielle had gotten the hang of both styles very fast. She preferred English because the saddle was so thin, compared with the Western one, that she said she felt she was riding bareback.

Shock of shocks, Vida preferred the support of the Western

saddle and had even gone cantering on Pepino for the first time. It had been an accident, but she hadn't panicked and was able to bring him to a halt without a problem. Brielle, for all her talk about wanting to learn all the gaits, got nervous when Leilani's trot became a little too fast for her taste and raised her knees.

"Now let your body flow with the movement," Kimber said. "Remember, it's one progression of the movement into another."

"It's so much to keep in mind," Brielle said.

"But you're doing it, Brielle!" Kimber said, ever the optimist. "You've come a long way from your first lesson."

Encouraged, Brielle smiled and led Leilani toward the top of the arena to start her round again.

Chelsie and Caro chuckled. Brielle had the impression that she could only start new moves from a certain spot, no matter how many times Kimber told her otherwise.

Brielle smacked her lips and made kissing sounds and Leilani started walking, and her steps sped up until she was gently trotting. Seamlessly, Brielle started posting the trot.

"I got it!" she cheered, but then Leilani slowed down.

Brielle started the sequence again.

In the meantime, Carolina leaned toward Chelsie and asked, "No idea about who the suit guy might be?"

Carolina had told her about the phone call with Loretta, and one thing had led to another until they were deep in speculations.

Chelsie looked up and gazed around them as if she were half expecting to see him crouching behind a tree. Unlike other classes in which Brielle's mom had stayed to watch, this time, there was no one around. The day was cloudy, carrying the promise of rain, and the girls had decided they'd had plenty of pool time for the week.

Still, Chelsie covered her mouth with her hand before she too leaned in toward Carolina and said, "No. But I saw the envelope and recognized the logo of the boarding school Loretta might attend in the fall."

"Might?"

Chelsie shrugged one shoulder.

Carolina jumped in her seat as if she was now getting pumpkin hives in her behind. "You mean it's not a done deal she's going?"

"Like I said, she hasn't told me anything about it—"

"But she's your friend!" Carolina interrupted her.

"I know! That's why I'm sort of hurt she hasn't told me anything. Even if she had, I feel a little stuck in the middle between you two sometimes. Even if you have made up, sort of." Chelsie bumped Caro's shoulder as if to soften what she said.

Carolina sobered up. "I'm sorry, Chels. I hate that I made you feel like that, in the middle."

Chelsie elbowed her. "Don't look so disappointed! Loretta hasn't told me anything, but Tessa did."

Carolina's eyes widened. She was desperate for Chelsie to tell her what she knew, but she didn't want to pressure her more. Chelsie laughed, probably at the look of impatience on Carolina's face.

The sounds carried to the other side of the arena, where both Vida and Brielle looked in their direction. Kimber cleared her throat in warning.

Carolina and Chelsie ducked sheepishly.

"What's up with that school?" Caro finally blurted. "Please tell me before I faint."

"Okay," Chelsie whispered. "At one of the first competitions we went to this summer, a recruiter from that fancy school saw Loretta, and I guess they loved her potential, or whatever. Ever since, the recruiter has been trying to get her to move there. To Montana!"

Carolina tried to absorb all the words. An opportunity like this was exactly what Loretta had wanted all her life. Or at least, it had been back when she and Carolina had been friends.

"So what's the deal with it? And why was this guy here at the ranch?"

"I'm not sure why Loretta didn't jump at the opportunity, but the more they insist, the more she's distanced herself from competitions and even coming to the barn."

"I've noticed," Carolina said. Just the night before, she'd helped Tessa muck Poseidon's stall since Bracken had to go home early. They hadn't exchanged a word about Loretta though.

"As to why the guy was here?" Chelsie rummaged in her pocket and took something out. "Here."

She held out the envelope Carolina had seen in her dad's

hands. Caro's hand shook with nerves as she took it. The paper was heavy, fancy, with a scrolled letterhead that read *Stillwater Equestrian Academy*.

"Stillwater?" she said with a snort, but she was curious.

"See for yourself," Chelsie said.

The letter was brief. It took Carolina a little while to interpret the formal wordiness, but it was nothing more than a request for a meeting with Heather about the Unbridled Dreams program.

"What do they want to know?" Carolina's mouth had gone dry. "Do they want to take it away from us like all the developers buying up all the orchards and ranches?"

Chelsie pressed her lips in a thin line. "I don't know. But no one is going to take our home from us."

"Thanks, Chels," Carolina said, hoping her friend felt the gratitude inside her.

Chelsie draped an arm over her shoulder.

Carolina looked Chelsie in the eyes and asked, "But even if they won't take the ranch from us, what if they want to take *you*? Would you move to that school too?"

Chelsie's face blushed deep red. To her, even hiding some

details was lying, and she never said something she didn't mean. After almost a year together, Carolina knew that Chelsie would strive to say only what she thought was the absolute truth.

She couldn't wait to go to middle school with Chelsie. But if Chelsie wanted to go to that equestrian school, then who was Carolina to ask her not to?

She held her breath.

"All these months, you can't imagine how much I've missed my dad," Chelsie said. "I miss our home in California. The life we had. But it's impossible to go back in time. I guess home means something different than what I always thought." She swallowed like she had a knot in her throat. Carolina held her hand.

Chelsie continued, "For the longest time, home was with both my parents together, but they weren't happy. Then we moved in with Aunt Bernice, but I didn't belong in that world. I couldn't even play music after eight o'clock or she'd be upset."

Carolina realized she rarely asked Chelsie about her life before Paradise.

"And then, we arrived here. And I found a sister, and like

sisters, sometimes we fight. But I feel at home after a long time," she said softly. "I still want to be with my dad, though, and when I visit him, I'll feel at home wherever he is. Home is . . . it changes, you know?"

"Sometimes it's not a physical place," Carolina said.

"It's where your heart is," Chelsie said, smiling through tears.

"My heart is with my family and the horses," Carolina said.

"Same," replied Chelsie. She pressed Carolina's hand. "I'm staying here at Paradise for however long I can."

Carolina didn't know what to say back, but that was okay. The two girls turned again to the riding lesson.

Vida started posting. Slowly. Briefly. But her form was perfect. Brielle trotted back to her favorite spot at the top of the arena and posted nearly all the way around the ring.

"Yay!" cheered Carolina and Chelsie, jumping up and down on the picnic table. The table wobbled, and they quickly got down, giggling.

In the arena, Vida let out a "Yeehaw!" of pure joy.

Reaching a goal is a special kind of magic. You feel invincible—like anything before you is within reach. That's how Carolina, Chelsie, Vida, and Brielle felt when the two new riders got the hang of posting the trot.

Sure, it wasn't the canter or the gallop that Brielle had been dreaming of, but this kind of victory was a thousand steps in the right direction. The adrenaline filled them all with a possibility that stretched until Carolina's much awaited birthday.

18

Cowboy Pool

For her twelfth birthday, Carolina received a present she had never expected.

Seeing how much she loved cooling off at the rec center, her dad and Tyler had repurposed one of the old stock water tanks leftover from when Mr. Parry kept cattle for a brief time. They couldn't move it from its spot at the south end of the property, but they made a few special improvements.

Together, they'd transformed it into a real aboveground pool, complete with a pump and filter, and a ladder so the girls could easily climb in. Its location by the creek and a cluster of weeping willows was perfect. Still within easy distance to the house, but far enough from the horses to prevent them from turning it into one of their watering troughs.

"Now you own a proper cowboy pool!" Tyler exclaimed, proud of his work.

"More like a resort!" Carolina exclaimed, floating on her back.

Now this was a proper paradise.

After trying out the temperature of the water and the depth of the tank, Carolina announced it was the perfect opportunity to teach Chelsie how to swim.

"Before the rec center closes for the season, we'll all jump from the diving board, okay?" she said. They had a few weeks for Chelsie to feel confident enough to try a cannonball. The rec center closed on Labor Day, right before school started.

Chelsie rolled her eyes like she doubted she'd be ready, but Brielle said, "Step by step you get to the big goals, right?"

"Right," said Vida.

Chelsie had no chance to argue after that.

JC and Tyler were nearby, working on fixing the wire fence that separated their ranch from the neighbor's. They didn't want the sheep to crash the swimming party either. At least that was the reason they'd given the girls, who insisted they didn't need babysitters.

Chelsie was the last to get in the chin-high, warm water.

"You can let go, Chels," Brielle said. "It's not that deep."

Chelsie was taller than Brielle, and her feet easily touched the ground, but she still held on to the rim of the tank. She'd applied so much sunscreen on her face that she looked like a ghost.

"Why do you hate freckles, Chelsie? Everyone loves them. Some people get them tattooed," Carolina said. "The other day Bracken was playing with his mom's phone and showed me a bunch of selfies he took with a filter that made it look like he had freckles."

"More freckles, you mean," said Vida, laughing. Her rainbow-dyed hair fanned around her face when she floated on her back.

"More freckles, yes. He looked adorable. As do you," said Caro.

Chelsie motioned to Tyler and JC, and said, "I don't want to be all wrinkly when I'm a grandma."

"My grandma is all wrinkly and she's beautiful," Carolina said.

Mortified, Chelsie hid underwater, but only for five

seconds because she was laughing so much at the outraged face Carolina had made.

"That's not what I meant!" Chelsie said when she came back up to the surface.

"I'm going to tell Abuela Ceci!" Carolina threatened, splashing her with water. Soon, the four of them were splashing water in all directions, and Chelsie swam away.

Surprised, Vida exclaimed, "Wait . . . What?"

"Are you sure you don't know how to swim?" asked Brielle.

"Yes. I mean, yes, I'm sure I don't know how to swim," said Chelsie. "We lived in an apartment, and my mom was so busy we never went to the rec center or the apartment pool. I guess, it's one of those things that slipped through the cracks."

"But maybe you know more than you think. Come here, do this," Carolina said, showing Chelsie how to turn on her back and float.

Vida and Brielle counted. Chelsie floated for a full minute.

"You're doing it!" Carolina exclaimed.

Brielle and Carolina stood by her sides and helped her float on her tummy, and then Vida showed her how to move her arms. When she thought too hard, Chelsie moved slowly and awkwardly, but when she relaxed, she started to slice through the water.

"You're a natural!" exclaimed Caro when Chelsie made it from one end of the tank to the other.

"Bravo, Chelsie!" Tyler said from the fence, and he clapped.

"Yeehaw!" exclaimed JC.

In that moment, JC's radio broke through the celebration, startling everyone. He answered, but Carolina couldn't tell what he was saying. He glanced up at the girls, and they all reacted to the worry flashing in his eyes as if it were a fire alarm. There was no time to panic. Only to take action.

Carolina got out of the tank and ran to his side, water dripping from her swimsuit, and the hard prairie grass prickling her legs. She didn't even care if it too gave her an allergic reaction. "What's wrong?"

Tyler and JC exchanged a look. "It's Shadow. Kimber wants us to come as fast as we can."

This wasn't how Carolina had expected to celebrate her birthday, but she didn't even think.

As if they'd rehearsed a rescue plan, they all got on the back of the cart and headed back to the ranch.

· ∪ ·

Like their moods, the day had turned cloudy. Even the stables seemed gloomier than usual, but there was a light shining in Shadow's stall. Flip-flops squeaking and squelching on the cement floor, the girls made their way to the Arabian.

Dr. Rooney, Kimber, and Heather were chatting in soft voices when the girls arrived in a whirlwind of concern for him.

Heather looked up and she tried to smile but her eyes were so sad, Carolina's heart fell to her stomach like a lead ball.

"What's wrong?"

"It's time for him to have the surgery, love," Heather said.

"Why now?" Carolina asked. She had thought they had more time.

"The vet in Boise had a cancellation in his schedule. If we can get Shadow there now, he'll have a better chance of recovering before the weather turns and makes it harder on his joints."

"Besides, his limping is becoming worse," Caro's dad said. "I'm afraid that if we don't have the procedure done now, his front legs will get injured. His body is trying to compensate, but the pressure is too much for those limbs too."

"He's been agitated because he's in lots of pain, poor Shadow," Dr. Rooney said. "We need to calm him down first, so he doesn't struggle on the drive." He was a quiet, reserved man. But he loved animals, especially horses. He'd been a childhood friend of Mr. Parry and knew every corner of Paradise since it had been his playground when he was a little boy. He too was part of their family, the family of the heart, the one you get to choose to love.

"What about the money?" Carolina asked. "We're still short a few hundred dollars."

What if all their efforts had been for nothing?

Sometimes you work for a goal, and do everything right, and then it's not enough to get to the finish line. It was so unfair. But like Abuela Ceci said, everything would be okay in the end, and if things weren't okay, that meant it wasn't the end.

Heather pressed her hand to her chest as if to slow her heart. "Your mom is going through the accounts. We're going to try to make it work."

Carolina knew the adults wouldn't say anything else about money in front of them.

"What does he need?" Chelsie asked, peering into the stall.

Heidi peeked at her friend from her stall beside him. There was so much love in her eyes, as if she was trying to send him strength.

If Carolina felt powerless in this situation, what did the horses feel, at the mercy of everyone, unable to control even where their home would be? She couldn't imagine.

"He needs to be hydrated all night," Dr. Rooney said. "He needs to be calm, so his stomach settles a little."

Chelsie and Carolina nodded. Brielle and Vida stood to the side, whispering, eyes shiny with tears.

Horses are emotion sponges. So many people experiencing fear and anxiety couldn't be good for Shadow.

"Let's go up to my house," Carolina said.

As the adults talked more about the surgery, the girls ran to change and wait for Vida's mom to pick her and Brielle up.

"We'll just get ready to watch Shadow all night," Carolina said when Vida asked what she was going to do.

"Chelsie," Brielle said before she got in her mom's car.

"Please text me with any updates, okay? Even if there's nothing we can do, we can at least send good vibes."

Carolina hugged her friends. They smelled of sunshine and sunblock. How strange for a day to start so wonderfully and end so terribly.

But that was life.

Carolina and Chelsie headed to the big barn for the longest night of their lives.

19

Big Goals, Little Steps

Every horse at Paradise, in the little barn and the big stables, seemed to sense one of their own was in pain. They were all subdued in their stalls.

Tyler, who would drive Shadow to Boise, was sleeping since he had a long road and lots of work ahead of him.

Carolina and Chelsie had volunteered for the task of keeping Shadow company throughout the night. The girls took turns checking that Shadow's hydrating IV was okay and patting his head as he lay on his side. To any other person, he might have looked like he was sleeping, but Carolina recognized that he was in pain. A part of him must have known that they were trying to help him feel better because he complied with every instruction and stayed still.

For the first time in his life, at least the time that Carolina had known him, he didn't fight them.

"Oh, my sweetheart!" she said, when he tried to nuzzle her hand.

She and Chelsie stayed awake all night, sometimes dozing against the hard wooden walls, sometimes cuddling the big, restless horse. They set an electric lantern by the stall door and shared worried glances in the dim, eerie lighting. Papi came every couple of hours to make sure they were okay. Carolina tried hard not to think about whether they had all the money for the surgery and post-op care. For some reason, she had it in her mind that if Shadow could get through this, he could make it through anything.

But when the sun started rising above the mountains, and the first rays of light peeked over Shadow's stall door, fear finally overtook her. She bit her lip so she wouldn't start crying as footsteps approached the stalls. It was her dad.

"You're going to be okay, Shadow," Carolina said. The words were as much to comfort herself as him.

"Ready?" Papi asked. He had dark, tired bags under his eyes. He'd been through this heartache with so many other horses before but watching them suffer was never easy. "Abuela Ceci lit a candle for him," he said, kissing Carolina on the top of her head. "Now we can only hope for the best."

As if in answer to Abuela Ceci's prayers, a car arrived.

"I'm sure that's Dr. Rooney," Papi said. "Do you want to let him know we're ready to get Shadow in the trailer?"

She nodded and ran out. But she was shocked to find it wasn't Dr. Rooney.

It was her friends Vida and Brielle. And next to them stood Loretta, Tessa, and Bracken.

Carolina was speechless.

"What?" she said when she could recover her voice, and then she remembered her manners. "I mean, good morning."

Loretta stretched out a hand and gave her a thick envelope.

"What is this?" Carolina asked.

"All these weeks, I've been trying to figure out if I'm going to go to Stillwater Academy or not. I've been so scared of the unknown, even if attending a riding academy like it is all I ever wanted. And then Shadow got sick." She sniffed. "He's not my horse, but he taught me a lot while Poseidon was learning his way around shows and stuff. I love him. I wished that I had a lot of money of my own to make sure he was okay. I helped Bracken make the brownies, and it wasn't enough. Then . . . I remembered the Five Bs. And what it says about not being able to do everything on our own. And about big goals being attained in little steps. So, I called everyone I knew and asked them to help." Loretta cleared her throat. "I love Paradise with all my heart. Even if one day I move away to reach the goals I've had for so long, I want to think that this place will continue. I'd love to think that the horses and the arena are still here, and that if I came back, it would be like coming home."

Chelsie placed a hand on Loretta's shoulder to encourage her to keep talking.

"My mom made some calls, and people from our neighborhood, the church, and even McAllister City donated to Shadow's fundraiser. We all pitched in what we could. I think we have enough money to get him taken care of. This ranch and the horses in it are part of Paradise, Carolina. We can't lose it or we lose our heart."

"Oh, Loretta," Carolina said, and surprising even herself, she hugged her ex-best friend. At first, Loretta's arms hung at her sides, and then she tentatively hugged Carolina back.

"Thank you," Chelsie said.

Carolina didn't know if she and Loretta would ever be friends like they used to be, but for now she was grateful that their common love for Paradise had brought them together.

· ∪ ·

Shadow and Tyler had been gone for hours. There was no point in waiting around the phone, so everyone busied themselves with work until they received an update, whatever it may be. Carolina was taking advantage of the time that he'd be gone to scour Shadow's stall with barn lime and leave it looking like new. Once she was satisfied that no fly would ever want to nest in it, she went on to polish his bridle, halter, and saddle.

"He won't be able to ride for a while," Kimber reminded her tenderly.

Carolina looked up and, lifting her chin, she said, "I know. But one day soon, he will be. And that day his tack will be ready for him. And so will I."

"Carolina!" she heard Chelsie's urgent voice calling from near the little barn. "He made it out of surgery! He's going to be okay!" Chelsie exclaimed, running toward Caro with her phone in her hand, her hair flying in all directions.

"Yes!" Carolina yelled, jumping up and down.

And it was proof that even Luna the cat was happy with the news because she didn't bother to remind Carolina to be quiet.

20

Parade of Friends

Shadow had to stay at the vet for a whole week, but finally, he came back home.

"He'll still need to rest alone in his stall, but we'll keep him company, right, Bracken?" Carolina asked, making sure the hay in the Arabian's stall was the freshest she could find.

"I'm ready with my books," Bracken said, pointing to his chair in a corner of the barn. He'd placed a precarious pile of books on top. It was so tall, Carolina knew sooner or later it would wobble and topple, but for now she wasn't going to say anything.

Bracken would learn his own lessons in their due time.

After three weeks of tender love and care, Shadow got the green light to go on short walks around the indoor arena. He was stubborn, and his recovery was proof of his determination to be the same old Shadow.

He might not be able to go on trail rides for a long time, but when the Paradise Day Parade arrived, Dr. Rooney determined that the Arabian would do just fine on level ground for a few city blocks, at most.

"Good thing the parade is super short," Chelsie said.

"Thank goodness!" Carolina said. She'd made her peace with the prospect of riding any other horse, but she was delighted with Shadow's progress. "Now let's go!"

All of Paradise, not just the ranch, was ready for the parade.

Their town had been through so much this year. But everyone was ready to celebrate another time around the sun.

Life at Paradise was hard sometimes, but oh, how beautiful it was!

Carolina felt regal in her brand-new turquoise boots and hat that Abuela Ceci had given her for her birthday. She'd put on an Unbridled Dreams shirt and was so happy to walk around her town and see so many people wearing the braided bracelets her friends had made all summer.

Even if the program ended with Brielle, they had accomplished so much! She still was the same Carolina as always and still got in trouble for being impulsive and intense. But she was learning how to love herself with her flaws and all.

She made her way to the back of the line where the staff and students from Paradise Ranch were getting ready for the parade.

Loretta was on Poseidon, looking beautiful in her riding outfit. She wore an Unbridled Dreams T-shirt too.

"I thought you'd be wearing your new school uniform," Carolina said.

Loretta didn't smile but her blue eyes softened. "Today I'm representing our ranch. Without it, I would've never been invited to Stillwater." And she walked off with Poseidon to join Tessa and Apollo.

As she got on Shadow, Carolina remembered last year's parade when she'd been the only kid, and then her dad, JC, Tyler, and Andrew had followed her as she waved the banner of Orchard Farms.

Now Kimber drove the truck that pulled a trailer decorated with balloons. Bracken, Cyrus, and their friends from story time, supervised by Molly Martin, were ready to throw candy to the public as they marched along Main Street.

Her eyes prickled with happiness seeing Tessa and Loretta, Gisella, Jaime, Chelsie, Brielle, Vida, and . . .

"Is that Rockwell?" she asked, seeing a familiar form on the other side of the crew. Was it really him? Carolina jumped from Shadow to run to her friend.

Rockwell's hair was much longer than the last time she'd seen him, and he was easily two heads taller than her. From the corner of her eye, she caught a peek of Bronco heading to the trailer where Bracken was crying with happiness at seeing his friend back for a visit.

"Hi, Caro," Rockwell said.

After a brief bout of shyness, she hugged him.

"How come you're here?" she asked, her heart pounding hard in her ears.

"My dad wanted to surprise Grandma Mae for her seventieth birthday tomorrow. I may have worked hard to convince him to arrive early for the parade." He still smiled shyly, and Carolina thought he looked more handsome than ever.

"I'm so happy you could make it. Napoleon's all dolled up. Look at him," she said, pointing to the end of their train.

"Oh wow," he said, seeing Napoleon's shiny mane braided in pretty ribbons like the rest of the horses. "I missed him so much."

"Go say hi, then," she said.

He ran to Napoleon and jumped on the saddle as if the months hadn't passed.

And then the parade started.

First down the street were the police officers on their motorcycles and the one cruiser in town, its lights flashing. Then went the EMT crew in the county's ambulance, and when the firefighters marched, the whole town cheered for their heroes. They had a small break from fighting fires in their area, but they were getting ready to head to Utah to help out with a fire in the Uinta Mountains.

Carolina clapped when it was the turn of Mr. Jones and the elementary school teachers, and then she beamed from ear to ear when Paradise Ranch was finally announced. They marched as one even though they hadn't practiced before.

She leaned down on the saddle to gently pat Shadow's neck. "Slow and steady. You're doing awesome, handsome."

Shadow flicked his ear and snorted, making her smile even wider.

She still didn't have a horse of her heart, but how her heart had expanded in just one year! Who knew how much more it would expand in the future, whatever life might bring?

Mr. Eves from the bookmobile waved at her from his little truck parked in the shade of the trees.

It was the happiest moment of her life and she wished she could put this feeling into a little bottle. If happiness had a scent, it would be a mix of the muskiness of horses, chlorine drifting from the pool, sunshine, and cotton candy from the vendors.

Carolina closed her eyes and soaked in the moment she had dreamed of for so long. She didn't know if they'd be able to bring more students to Unbridled Dreams. But no matter what, she was so happy with how much good it had done in their little part of the world!

21

Silver Linings

The festivities—the end-of-summer parade, Carolina's birthday, and Shadow's recovery—would not be complete without a final trip to the pool. Chelsie raced Jaime in laps until the group called them to the picnic table to have cupcakes.

Although it was still technically summer, the days were already shorter and a chill in the air announced the change of seasons. Up in the mountains, there were flashes of reds and golds from the leaves already turning.

"Although," said Vida, "what are we really celebrating? More snow? Back to school?"

"We're celebrating that we'll all be together in school this year," said Brielle. "Imagine how fun it will be!"

Carolina smiled. She looked away and saw Loretta, Tessa,

and a group of children eating pizza and laughing. They hadn't talked at the parade, and there were still things to resolve between them. But it was nice to see her happy and not with that frown that Carolina had started to think was Loretta's permanent face. Bracken said his sister would be leaving for her new school the following week.

Carolina was happy Loretta was following her dreams, or at least, she was trying them out to see if they still fit her.

By the time they went back home, the girls were exhausted, but never so much they couldn't say good-night to the horses. Carolina had wanted to move Shadow to the little barn, which was closer to the cottage, but he and Heidi had become such good friends, no one had the heart to separate them. Besides, there was no room for two more horses in the little barn. The baby horse would be born sometime at the end of September, and the big barn was the perfect place to keep mother and baby comfortable.

The girls headed to check on Shadow. Abuela Ceci was reading to him.

"When did you get here, Abuelita?" Carolina asked. "I didn't see you leave the parade."

Abuela Cecilia waved a hand in front of her face like she was shooing a pesky fly away and said, "Mr. Jones gave me a ride."

The silence that followed was like that which follows a thunderclap.

"Mr. Jones?" Chelsie asked, like always, the first one to recover. "Like, the principal?"

"Vida's grandfather?" blurted Carolina.

Abuela Ceci shook her head and a finger at them. "Now, now, we've known each other for years and are good friends. Who do you think tells me what my granddaughter and her friends are up to at school all year? Now that you're growing, I'll need to make friends with the middle school principal."

Chelsie and Carolina laughed, but Carolina wasn't sure Abuela was joking. In a way, it would be nice if she had more friends to keep her anchored in Paradise so she didn't go back to New Mexico with Tío Achilles and his family. But time would tell.

They'd had this conversation before, and Abuela Ceci must have understood what the scheming look on Caro's face meant. "Caro, you know this is my home too. But soon it will be time for me to return to my house, my plants, and your cousins. Don't worry, soon, you'll come to see me. The separation and wait won't last two years."

"You promise?" Carolina asked, holding up her pinky finger.

Abuela Ceci hooked hers in Caro's and said, "Promise."

Carolina sighed.

"Don't be dreading that moment now and sour the days we have left," her abuela said. "Remember the Five Bs: Be present!"

"They also say to plan for the future." Carolina turned to Shadow, who was leaning his forehead into Chelsie's petting. "How's our friend doing?"

As if he understood her words, Shadow neighed, showing his front teeth, and tossed his head to the side.

"I think he's saying he's good as new!" Chelsie said.

Carolina laughed and pressed her forehead against his nose. "I can't wait to get back on the trail with you, Shadow. We never did get to the top of Sleeping Princess Rock."

"We can still go in the fall," Chelsie said.

"But our goal was this summer!" Carolina complained.

"That's the thing with goals," Abuela said. "You can make

the plans, and prepare, and go step by step toward them. But sometimes, life will surprise you with a detour. And although Shadow's surgery was scary, look at the silver lining too."

Carolina thought and started counting good things with her fingers. "Unbridled Dreams brought the community together. I met new friends. More people than ever want to be part of Paradise. The best is that Shadow is healthy and officially part of Paradise forever." She paused before the what-ifs could drown out her happiness. For right now, for today, she'd accomplished everything she needed to.

"I learned how to embroider and now I can finally swim!" Chelsie said.

Abuela Ceci hugged her. "Yes, you did, mi amor. See? There are a lot of things to be grateful for."

Caro couldn't help herself and finally said, "I don't want to sound ungrateful, but it's hard not to be sad that we couldn't find a sponsor to keep funding Unbridled Dreams. Think of all the wonderful things we could still do."

"Well," Abuela Ceci said, setting her book down and smiling in a mischievous way that robbed Carolina of her breath. "About that . . ."

"What?" Chelsie exclaimed. "You look like you have a secret!"

Abuelita Ceci laughed. Her eyes were sparkling.

Carolina didn't want to get her hopes up, but she hoped for a miracle.

And a miracle is what they got.

"Your parents gave me the opportunity to tell you two the news. Unbridled Dreams found a sponsor after all," Abuela Ceci said. "They wanted to wait until it was official."

Carolina and Chelsie clasped hands as they listened attentively to the rest of the details.

It turned out that the riding school recruiter had been so impressed with their program and specifically the Five Bs, that he'd offered for Stillwater to sponsor students in exchange for being able to teach the Five Bs at the fancy school in Montana.

"Who would've thought our set of principles would travel so far?" Chelsie exclaimed with a dreamy look in her eyes.

Carolina's heart was too full of gratitude, and she just hugged her abuela under the watchful eye of Shadow.

22

The Beginning of the Journey

Gisella and Rockwell had just finished mucking the stalls in the little barn when they joined the rest of their friends to watch Brielle's last class.

Today it was raining, so they were holding Brielle's final class in the indoor arena.

A small crowd was waiting on the bleachers in the corner. Jaime and Vida looked like twins sitting on either side of Abuela Ceci. Everyone wanted to soak in time with her before she went back home the following week. Brielle's parents and her brother were chatting with Heather who looked radiant after going over the numbers from the previous year with Caro's mom. The good news hadn't stopped.

And then Kimber and Brielle finally entered the arena,

leading Marigold, and everyone clapped. It kind of felt like an end-of-year recital.

Chelsie and Carolina sat in the first row, holding hands, and beaming with pride at how much their program had grown. Yes, they had made a grave mistake that night they took Velvet out to train her, but in the spirit of looking at the silver lining, they wouldn't have gotten to this moment if it hadn't been for that night.

The love of Velvet had grown into love for all the horses and the students they had.

Carefully, Brielle went through the join-up. Marigold had been ready to start the class from the moment she'd stepped into the arena, and she followed Brielle's body language attentively. Then Brielle mounted and had Marigold walking like she was a show horse. They switched directions; they made patterns with the barrels. It was a beauty to see.

"She's using the English saddle!" Carolina noted in admiration.

Chelsie beamed at her. "Yes!"

And in a smooth fluid movement, Marigold started trotting and Brielle didn't freeze. She was fully in the moment, synchronized with the horse. She started posting for one, two, three turns around the ring.

"There she goes," whispered Carolina, her heart following the music of the trotting mustang.

"She's doing it!" said Chelsie, proud like a momma hen.

Kimber quietly directed Brielle's movements from the center of the arena, but it was clear their student knew each step that was coming next. She was firmly sat in the saddle, fully connected with Marigold.

When Brielle was done, Marigold looked like she was smiling. A glimpse of the wild horse she'd once been peeked from her eyes as Brielle threw her arms around her neck.

Carolina couldn't wait to tell Brielle about the email full of photos and videos of her that was waiting in her mom's inbox. She hoped it was the perfect memento of Brielle's first summer riding. She hadn't galloped Marigold the way she'd dreamed on day one. But Carolina could see on her face that all her accomplishments during the program were enough.

After all, this was only the beginning of the journey for a brand-new horse-crazy Brielle.

·⋃·

The night before seventh grade, Chelsie and Carolina went riding in the pasture by themselves. Tyler was finishing repairs on the little barn's roof and, from up there, kept an eye on them. There was nothing to worry about though. The girls were wearing their helmets and knew the place like the palms of their hands.

Where her thumb held her reins, Carolina felt the scar from the prickly apple thorn from the beginning of the summer. She was glad her body had finally pushed it out the week before.

In a way, it was like when she'd plucked out the thorn of her tension with Loretta. It had left a scar in her heart. Even when you forgive someone or ask for forgiveness, words leave scars as a reminder to be kinder next time.

"It's amazing that in just a year Velvet has mellowed out so much," Chelsie said. "My dad said that next month when he comes to visit, he'll teach us some polo."

Carolina turned to look at her with surprise. "Woah, cowgirl!" Marigold stopped, thinking Carolina was talking to her, and the girls laughed and urged their horses to keep on going toward the red sunset.

"That's so exciting!" Carolina said. "How come you didn't tell me before now?"

Chelsie laughed. "I just found out!"

"I can't wait to meet him," Carolina said, resisting the urge to wiggle with happiness in her saddle.

"Maybe one day . . . we could go visit him in Argentina," Chelsie said shyly.

Carolina could only grin in response. "And one day . . ." she said, "you'll beat me in a race, but today is not that day."

Chelsie smiled. "Is that a challenge?"

They were gone before either of them counted. Mustang and Thoroughbred ran through the grass, excited to let all their pent-up energy free.

Carolina held on tight with her legs and opened her arms, and when she looked to her side, Chelsie was doing the same. They were flying.

Later, after they'd put the horses to bed, they went out to the campfire the wranglers had built to say farewell to summer.

"Can we go up on the roof?" Carolina asked. Tyler had left the ladder and the painting platform.

"Yes," said Carolina's dad. "Just be careful."

"Always, Papi," she said.

He kissed her head and the girls headed up to the roof where they could see all around them to the valley. It wasn't the top of the mountain, but Sleeping Princess Rock wasn't going anywhere. They'd keep trying to ride up in the fall to catch the colors turn.

Tomorrow, they'd winterize the sprinkler system. Carolina was always sad when that moment arrived. But this time things were different.

"We'll all be new at school this year," she said, leaning against the slant of the roof.

Chelsie took a sip of her hot chocolate and nodded. Her eyes were twinkling. "It's going to be fun to get to know more people. Do you have your outfit chosen?"

Carolina laughed. Tomorrow she would grab a pair of jeans and one of her Unbridled Dreams T-shirts.

"I'll polish my boots," she said.

Chelsie laughed. She'd had her outfit ready for days and

days. Since the middle school was so far, they'd both be riding on the bus.

"Soon the baby will be born," Chelsie said.

"And we'll get more students."

"But now we have this moment. To more years in Paradise," Chelsie said, and they toasted with hot chocolate.

"To endless years in Paradise."

They had plans for the future, and they were excited. Who knew what detours they'd find along the way?

Acknowledgments

Thank you, Olivia Valcarce, for going on this wonderful journey with me! Horse Country would have never happened without your support and encouragement. I'm so proud of these books! We'll always have Paradise.

Thank you, Linda Camacho, for making all my dreams come true and for being the best agent in the world.

Thank you to the whole team at Scholastic: Aimee Friedman, Elisabeth Ferrari, Kelli Boyer, Stephanie Yang, Omou Barry, Elizabeth Parisi, Tiffany Colón, Rachel Feld, Kristin Standley, Mary Kate Garmire, Savannah D'Amico, and so many others. Thank you, Winona Nelson, for the gorgeous covers and illustrations!

Thank you also to the teachers and librarians for your wonderful work of loving and educating our children. You're heroes!

Thank you to my friends. You make my life magical! Veeda Bybee, Amparo Ortiz, Lindsey Leavitt, Ally Braithwaite Condie, Shannon Hale, Ann Dee Ellis, Giselle White, Mariana Vargas, Mariana Stephenson, Luciana Bustos, Tania Perez, Ana Margarita Raga, Andrea Taylor, and Denisse Dixon.

Thank you, Plot-Twister sisters: Kalie Chamberlain, Ellen Misner King, Jennifer Maughan, Jill Tucker, and Megan Jensen.

Thanks to Las Musas and the VCFA Harried Plotters.

Gracias a mi familia por todo el amor que me dan.

Most importantly, thank you, dear readers, for loving Caro, Chelsie, and the whole crew so much. Your messages keep me inspired and hopeful for the future. See you on the range!

HORSE COUNTRY

Welcome to Paradise Ranch,
where everyone can get a second chance.

#1: Can't Be Tamed

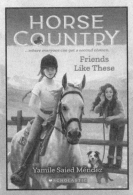

#2: Friends Like These

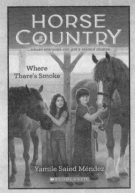

#3: Where There's Smoke

#4: No Place Like Home